Death in Driftless Hollow

Ben Tor

DREADFULLY CURIOUS

Cover Design by Evgeniia Gurcheva

Copy Editing by Lisa Gilliam

Proofreading by Lucy Littlejohns

Formatting by Dreadfully Curious

Copyright © 2026 by Ben Tor

All rights reserved.

First print and electronic edition: 2026

www.dreadfullycurious.com

www.bentorauthor.com

ISBN (paperback): 979-8-9941472-1-4

ISBN (ebook): 979-8-9941472-0-7

Prologue

Frozen branches lashed her arms, but Mara didn't dare stop. Not now. Her lungs burned, throat cinched as if stitched shut, legs stumbling as the trail curved.

Then—her foot snagged. She pitched forward, catching herself hard on one knee. A flat layer of sticks, snow-dusted and lashed with yellow paracord, lay almost flush with the trail.

Concealment.

She squinted, leaned, pulled at a corner.

The lattice peeled back with brittle snaps. Beneath, five feet down: sharpened stakes, their tips damp and blackened. A spool of rusted barbed wire coiled like a serpent. Past that, a pair of plow blades—old, heavy, dulled by years until someone had sharpened the edges bright again.

A pitfall.

Not an accident. Not nature.

Deliberate.

Fuck.

She dropped the cover, staggered upright, and ran.

The trail forked, splitting around a cluster of pines. She veered into the crook, branches thick enough to hide her, she hoped. Crouching low, she pressed back, breath slicing shallow through her teeth. Her muscles trembled with the effort to stay still.

Then—boots. Pounding through deep snow, relentless. A figure burst through the trees, hammering down the very trail she had just fled. Their breath tore ragged from their chest, head jerking back as though something stalked them.

Too far for a face—just motion, frantic and wrong.

Closer. Faster. Straight toward her.

Mara's pulse lashed. She pressed deeper into the fork, snowflakes clinging to her lashes. The figure's sprint looked aimed for her, as if they'd already marked her. If they weren't the killer, they'd need help.

She tried to brace for flight, but her body refused, trembling violently. Closer now—wild, uncoordinated, not even looking forward. And then the thought slammed her: They hadn't seen the pit.

Her throat clamped harder, strangling the cry before

it formed. If they'd built it, they'd skirt the edge. But their boots thundered straight down the center.

Humans help humans.

The urge came primal, brutal.

One second. Two.

They were almost on it.

Her voice ripped free, raw, cracking the silence.

"Stop!"

The figure's head snapped toward her. A beat of hesitation—then they surged faster, as if chased by something unseen.

Mara's hand tore at the air. "Stop!"

The false ground gave way. Wood snapped. Snow collapsed. The figure vanished with a sound so sharp it seemed to split the forest itself. Then the impact rose, layered and ugly: sticks splintering like bone, wire shrieking against flesh, and finally the blunt, wet crack of body against hardness—subdued, smothered, as the frozen earth swallowed the noise.

Silence flooded back, heavier than before. Only her breath proved the world still moved.

It cut through at last.

A guttural sound, faint and wet, not quite a word but something primal—life leaking out slow, stubborn, unwilling to be finished.

Whatever was down there was still alive.

Humans help humans, she thought, staggering toward the pit. Dr. Hill's voice, her own, something ancient braided between them.

“Uketamo.”
(I accept.)
Yamabushi tradition

Chapter 1

Mara tightened her grip on the wheel. Snow—no, sleet—slanted across the windshield, streaking beneath wipers that never caught up. The defogger wheezed, too hot, then too cold, until the glass blurred again.

The road was a thin ribbon of gravel between bare trees, just wide enough for one car. She imagined headlights rushing at her from the opposite direction, nowhere to swerve. Or worse—something older, slower, a horse-drawn carriage rattling out of the Wisconsin woods like she'd slipped back a century.

CarPlay chirped directions in its calm, not-so-synthetic voice, though the "No Signal" badge had glared for miles. GPS was supposed to work without service—satellite magic, she guessed—but it hadn't stopped her from looping what felt like the same half-circle of rural backroads, over and over.

She couldn't shake the thought that she'd botched the address. Maybe when she copied it from the confirmation email, one of those nonsense rural numbers—N16482—got scrambled. She saw it clear in her mind, digits swimming, just enough to convince her she'd done it wrong.

Her stomach knotted. She should stop, cancel the route, reenter it. Double-check. Triple-check. Except—no bars. Without service, retyping it meant staring at a blank screen. Didn't it? She wasn't even sure the map would stay alive if she touched anything.

The voice repeated itself, patient, certain.

"Continue straight."

Straight where?

The road narrowed, gravel overtaking asphalt, sloping into fields blurred by half rain, half snow. Her eyes flicked from windshield to screen to rearview and back again.

Nothing. Just her.

Her chest locked. Breath shallow. She hunched toward the wheel, nausea rising. Did I get the wrong address? Did I make a wrong turn? She imagined herself circling forever, fuel burning low, snow thickening, no signal, no help.

The voice chirped again.

"In two hundred feet, turn right."

Her laugh cracked out loud, brittle, half mad.

Sure. Right fucking where?

Her back ached, eyes straining, nausea climbing—panic winding sharp and stupid through her chest.

Six months ago, she couldn't drive at all. Then came Dr. Hill and his cursed "exposure" work. *Short drives. One block. Then two. Then merge onto a highway and sit with it.* Now she was three states from home. Alone. In February.

The symptoms arrived anyway—fast, merciless, like weather breaking. Her vision narrowed, the windshield shrinking to a tunnel. The steering wheel rattled in her grip, lane-keeping jittery, as though the car itself shook with her.

She felt cold sweat slicked along her ribs. Her thighs locked, bracing for a crash that hadn't happened. The hiss of wipers grew deafening, sleet like static on her ears.

Once, months ago, she'd been so certain she'd pass out behind the wheel she wet herself, trembling as semis roared past like metal beasts. This wasn't that bad —not yet. But the memory lurched up in a half gag anyway.

Her hands clutched tighter, as if the wheel were the last thread keeping her alive. Her heart galloped, too fast, too hard. Louder than tires, louder than wipers.

Is this a heart attack? If she fainted, if she let go, she would crash out here alone. Probably die.

The car swayed with her fear, harder than it should have. A phantom wobble whispered: flat tire, blown axle, you'll lose control.

Her body believed it. Every motion, every hiss of sleet. Her body believed everything.

Then—*there.* A square post, paint chipped, topped with a wooden triangle:

Driftless Cabin Co. →

Mara let out a sound, half laugh, half sob. The car rolled smoother as she turned. Maybe she hadn't blown a tire after all. Maybe she was the wreck.

Another sign appeared a hundred yards in, beneath a timber overhang. She braked. A mounted map displayed six cabins along a looping one-way road, each with a number and name.

She rolled down her window and tapped her phone for the text she'd received earlier that day:

Your Driftless Cabin retreat is waiting. You'll be staying in Sophie – Cabin 3.

Use keycode 2137 to enter.

Reception is limited at camp. Disconnection is part of the experience. Welcome to your stay!

Number three. Sophie. Pretty, though the name carried a taste Mara couldn't quite swallow—ironic, maybe, or too close to history she'd rather not revisit. Still, she let it be. The cabin was in the middle, tight between the others. Snug. Secure.

Beside the map hung a metal phone box with a placard:

For a personal welcome, ring the groundskeeper.

"No, thank you," Mara muttered. Relief poured through her shoulders like warm water. She put the car in park.

For the first time since leaving the interstate, she breathed all the way out. Her grip slackened. The world widened, slow, grudging, as if pried open. Her eyes stung. A jagged laugh shuddered loose, broke into a sob she hadn't known she was holding.

It counted. She was here, upright, breathing.

She drew in damp pine and thawing soil. The sleet softened into wet flakes. Pulse slowed, leaving that strange emptiness—panic's comedown. Flu-like good sick—that strange, swirling emptiness panic left behind. Almost euphoric. Nothing in the world relieved like terror draining away.

This was it. Three nights. Proof she could do it—be it—whatever Dr. Hill thought she could be.

The woods shimmered around her, briefly trans-formed. The sleet had eased into heavy flakes that drifted sideways on the wind, pale sheets sweeping across the pines. Every branch wore a glimmering crown of snow, each trunk banded in white as if the whole forest had been carved from sugar. But with green pine and yellow grass emerging like a hint of spring.

It was beautiful, almost impossibly so—a postcard no one else was around to see.

Then she glanced into her rearview. The tire tracks she'd left only minutes ago, the proof that she had come this way, were gone. Wind, slush, and snow had already smoothed them flat, erased her presence as if she'd never been there.

The thought landed: She could vanish here, folded into the woods until no one remembered she'd tried.

It was irrational. She told herself that. Still, her stomach knotted. Relief only held so long against the knowledge that she hadn't seen another human being in hours. No headlights, no farm trucks, no figures on porches. Nothing.

Isolation pressed in from every side.

She exhaled hard, willing herself to take the gift of shelter as enough. At least she'd reached the cabins. She'd have four walls, a roof, even heat. She could ride the storm out. But the snow thickened as she watched, and she suspected what her gut already knew: She wouldn't be driving back out on those roads until the weather cleared. That could be tomorrow. Or it could be days.

Mara put the car in gear, rolled up her window, and followed the loop road toward Cabin 3.

Sophie.

Chapter 2

The loop wound narrow, one-way, gravel pressed dark and wet. Now and then it widened into cutouts, single-car alcoves tucked in the trees, each paired with a cabin. A design choice, she realized. Guests parked in hollows; the cabins stayed untouched, elevated, preserved in their solitude.

Cabin 1 appeared first. Black walls, clean lines, set uphill beyond a shallow rise of patchy grass. From the cutout below, the slope was short but steep—climbing it meant lifting feet, catching breath. The cabin felt earned, like an escape hatch just out of reach of the road.

A sign near the cutout:

Nature Trail →

Beside it, a bench sat beneath half-melting snow. It faced nothing at all. Still, it suggested a pause—or a wait.

Cabin 2 came after a long, hushed stretch. Again uphill. This one angled away, turned from the road like it guarded its privacy. The cutout below was empty. No tire tracks, no footprints. Only the small black cube cabin itself, half-concealed by pines.

Her heart ticked faster. She wanted Sophie. Cabin 3.

It appeared not long after, tucked behind a stand of trees that opened into a clearing. Again uphill, but separated this time by a shallow ditch. A wooden footbridge spanned the gap, absurdly quaint against the cabin's matte-black cube. Its railings gleamed with wet snow, planks dark with damp.

Beyond it, little Sophie rose, her windows reflecting the gray February sky.

Mara cut the engine. Silence fell. The patter of sleet seemed distant now, muffled beneath a heavier stillness. She opened the door, stepped out. Boots sank into soft gravel. The ditch, the slope, the tiny bridge—already she felt removed from the road, standing at the threshold of a second, smaller world.

The air smelled of wet earth and pine. Snow sloughed from branches with the hiss of melting. Patches of yellow grass leaned among green needles and rising fog. For a moment, it felt older than Wisconsin—bog-colored, strange.

And then the silence deepened. A silence that said: *You are alone now.*

She bent forward into the walk, every step punctuated by the crunch of black gravel mixed with slush. It was a layered sound—hard stone breaking under her heels and, beneath it, the soft squelch of wet, almost like confused rain trying to decide whether to fall or stay. She liked the sound; it was strangely satisfying.

The air itself felt undecided.

A green line of melt ran under white crust, moss bleeding through where wind scoured bare patches, while fresh flakes drifted sideways across her coat.

Spring and winter were locked in an argument, warm snap against cold snap, each winning in turns, with no clear victor. Mara knew storms like this. They never negotiated. The snow would win until it didn't. It reminded her of panic—two seasons of herself clashing, each certain, each merciless.

The ambivalence unsettled her. One moment her breath fogged thick, heavy in the air; the next it vanished almost cleanly, carried off by a brief push of mild wind.

Melt whispered from tree limbs, a false promise of thaw, only to harden again in the next gust. It felt less like weather than a feud. And she was caught in it, a trespasser walking across a line where seasons overlapped.

Snap.

Mara froze.

Twenty yards ahead, a doe grazed where snow thinned to yellow grass. Beside her, a fawn nosed through the melt and snow, tugging stems.

The doe lifted her head. Stared at Mara. Dead-on. Ears pricked, body motionless, only the flare of breath in cold air.

The eyes—black, liquid, impossibly deep. At twenty yards, prey eyes shouldn't mean anything. But something in them pulled. A shine catching weak light, bending it inward, bottomless. Not dull animal beads but wells, polished by millennia of fear. Staring into them felt like leaning over a cavern rim, dizzy at the drop.

The fawn chewed frozen grass, the sound sharp in the hush. The mother never blinked. The gaze held— steady, patient, unreadable. Mara's chest tightened, breath snagged, though some part of her remembered this look before language, before cities.

Ancient. Eyes that had measured humans by fire-light before history learned a word.

The woods hushed again until her breath was the only sound.

The moment stretched. Then, as if nothing had

passed between them, the doe moved. She turned, angling her flank.

And Mara's awe cracked to horror.

The hide she now saw was wrong. Pocked and swollen—dark nodules bulging beneath fur like sick marbles. Some small and slick, others ballooned into grotesque lumps, crusted, split. A colony of growths gnawed into the animal's side.

Against the sleek grace of the rest of her, the deformity jarred like rot on a perfect apple.

The fawn butted her leg, unbothered. The doe twitched an ear, unconcerned. Another step, another shift of angle, and more came into view—knots ruptured black, some weeping, shapes that seemed to writhe until she blinked them still.

Her throat dampened with that acrid pre-vomit wet. The spell of those ancient eyes snapped.

Beauty gutted by ruin.

Mara lingered until mother and fawn vanished into pine and snow. When she finally crossed the quaint wooden bridge toward Sophie, it gave a single, deliberate creak beneath her boots—a sound too sharp in the silence, as though the place had taken note of her.

Her skin crawled, carrying the deer imprint—grace welded to blight, burned into her vision.

Small Sophie loomed close now, quiet and watchful at the top of the slope. Black walls sheened with wet, her angles sharp against the blur of trees, like a structure pulled from some future and dropped here by mistake. A faint glow of the glass storm door reflected the sky, broken by snow slants and the vague outline of Mara herself climbing toward it.

She paused.

The woman reflected back was middle-aged, no longer soft around the edges of youth, but not undone either. Lines marked her brow, shadows deepened beneath her eyes, yet she looked... fine. Better than fine, considering. *No kids. No partner, anymore. No one waiting back home.* Just a backpack stuffed with oats, a leaky pen, and two old books she wasn't sure she even believed in anymore.

She was here. Alone, yes, but not beaten. Six months ago, she'd barely stepped beyond her own apartment, unable to face even a grocery aisle without panic tightening her throat. A year ago, the thought of crossing three states into snowy forest would have been laughable. And yet here she was.

Alive.

Upright.

Doing it.

The pride stirred something warm in her chest, but doubt edged it quickly. Was she strong enough for whatever came next? Was courage just a word she'd borrowed without paying for?

She had prepared for the possibility of nothing happening. That, more than anything, had felt like the risk.

In the reflection, she saw the stormy sky roll behind her, clouds dragging low, snow weaving sudden thick curtains across the pines. Sophie's glass shimmered with it, as though the cabin held a second, storm-snarled world inside.

Her hand found the keypad. She pressed the code. The lock gave, small and decisive.

The snow fell harder. The tracks she'd made on the bridge were already filling in. Mara understood, in a quiet, heavy way: She would not be leaving this place until the storm itself released her.

Sophie had her now.

Chapter 3

Dr. Hill:

Before we begin—what would be
most useful today?

Mara:

The nights. And… the knife thing.
I hate saying it.

Dr. Hill:

Thank you for saying it anyway.
That's a step toward it, not away.
When the knife fear shows up,
what does your mind say?

Mara:

People shouldn't have intrusive
thoughts about stabbing the
woman they love.

Dr. Hill:

You'd be surprised, Mara. Lots of
people have thoughts like this—
pushing others down stairs,
swerving into traffic, shouting at
funerals, dropping a baby. The
brain alarms where you care
most.

Mara:

[…]

Dr. Hill:

What does your mind say?

Mara:

What if I stab her? I don't want to.
I just… what if I do?

Dr. Hill:

And your body?

Mara:

My chest tightens. Hands tingle.
The room feels… not real. Like I
could do it.

Dr. Hill:

So your body shouts too—tight
chest, tingling hands, the room
shifting. Notice that. You're here,
breathing.

Mara:

But why is it saying danger?

Dr. Hill:

Your brain is identical to people
who lived fifty thousand years
ago. What did people do then?

> **Mara:**
>
> Hunt. Run. Stay alive. Not die.

Dr. Hill:

Exactly. That wiring is still yours.

> **Mara:**
>
> It feels like I'm dangerous.

Dr. Hill:

That's a thought. But a thought
isn't a command.

> **Mara:**
>
> It's weather. A storm.

Dr. Hill:

A storm.

> **Mara:**
>
> But we can't control the weather.

Dr. Hill:

What can we influence?

> **Mara:**
>
> Ourselves. How?

Dr. Hill:

Two pieces. First: the words. Try
this—"I'm having the thought that
I'll stab her."

Mara:

...I'm having the thought that I'll stab her.

Dr. Hill:

How does that land?

Mara:

It feels like words. Not... like a plan.

Dr. Hill:

Good. That's defusion. That's the move we're practicing. The thought stays, but you unhook a little. Second: We practice being willing—exposure. We'll step into the scene your mind fears, safely, and stay with it instead of running. That's how your body learns it doesn't need to scream quite so loud. Want to try, just in our head?

Mara:

Yes.

Dr. Hill:

Close your eyes if you'd like. Picture the kitchen. The sink. A chef's knife in the basin, the big one your girlfriend leaves after cutting tomatoes. See it?

Mara:

...Yeah.

Dr. Hill:

Tell me about it.

                    Mara:

        Black handle… knicks in it. Steel
        blade. Smears of red.

Dr. Hill:

Notice it. Let the details sharpen
—the shine, the nicks in the
handle. And the air?

                    Mara:

        Garlic. Tomato. Acidic. Like iron,
        almost sweet.

Dr. Hill:

Good. Let that smell in—that's
here, that's now. And alongside it,
notice your body. What's it doing?

                    Mara:

        My chest is tight. My hands want
        to hide the knife. Throw it away.

Dr. Hill:

Good noticing. Say the line.

                    Mara:

        I'm having the thought that I'll
        stab her.

Dr. Hill:

Again.

Mara:

I'm having the thought that I'll
stab her.

Dr. Hill:
And your choice?

Mara:

…I'm choosing not to.

Dr. Hill:
Beautiful. Stay here. The knife
shines. The smell lingers. And you
stay, breathing. She steps into the
room. She says your name—
Mara. Notice her voice. Notice
your urge. And notice you're still
here. She's here. Both unharmed.

Mara:

I'm still here.

Dr. Hill:
That's courage—not feeling safe,
but staying anyway. If your fear
had a job, what would it be?

Mara:

To stop me from messing
everything up. To keep me…
belonging.

Dr. Hill:

And it's working too hard. Over-
watching. But even while afraid,
you can choose. That's the
muscle we're building.

Mara:

We fear less when we stop trying
to avoid it.

Dr. Hill:

That's it. Exposure isn't "feeling
safe." It's "being willing while
afraid."

Dr. Hill:

So—what do you want this
courage for?

Mara:

To go on the trip. To not scare her.
To sleep.

Dr. Hill:

Values. Let them steer. What's
one small exposure step toward
that life?

Mara:

Leave a knife on the counter while
we cook. Five minutes. Tell her
I'm practicing.

Dr. Hill:

Perfect. If the thought returns?

Mara:
I'm having the thought… and I'm
choosing not to act.

Dr. Hill:
Exactly. Message me one word
after: done.

Chapter 4

She woke with sensations that felt almost borrowed, like someone else's dream had leaked into her sleep.

The cabin smelled of old pine, processed lumber, and faint woodsmoke. Frost clung to the massive window that took up nearly an entire wall of the tiny cabin, a lace of white against the dim light.

For a moment she just breathed it in. It was nothing like the muted air of her ordinary apartment, where paint, carpet, and drywall dulled everything into the same faint chemical hush. She remembered it like a weight—a place where nothing belonged to her.

Here, the air had teeth—sap and resin cutting through it, sharp and clean. It was startling if you weren't used to it, like stepping outside after weeks of stale heat and finally tasting cold air. The walls themselves seemed to exhale.

Mara sat up, tugged her sweater close, and tried to recall when she'd last slept so hard. The strangeness of it struck her. She felt something good. Human again. Grounded.

Mara felt *well.*

Sleep had always been fragile for her, a thread that snapped the moment her body rehearsed its alarms—heart racing, chest tightening, the certain belief she'd die before morning. Even her ex-girlfriend once joked she "practiced death every night"—a line Mara never forgave. And yet here, in this borrowed cube in the woods, she'd slept deeply. Without aid, without pacing the floor or forcing herself to count breaths. The irony almost made her laugh: After years of insomnia in her own apartment, she'd finally slept like a baby in the middle of nowhere.

She thought of the night before, when she'd unpacked the welcome kit and found the cabin's sly features: a box labeled Fireside S'mores tucked neatly on the shelf with matches and a pair of skewers. Graham crackers, chocolate, a small bag containing exactly four marshmallows.

She'd made one, crouched over the little fire ring outside until the marshmallow blistered and sagged. It had tasted preposterously good, part sugar, part victory.

Her fingers stuck together afterward, and she'd been tempted to lick them like a kid but stopped, embarrassed even alone. It felt like a trick meant for families, but it worked on her too.

For ten minutes she'd sat grinning in the cold, sticky-fingered, not thinking of panic at all.

The cabin itself impressed her more than she wanted to admit. Barely larger than a single-room RV—bed, small stove and sink, a narrow bathroom tucked into one wall—but everything fit. Every inch served some purpose. Drawers folded out of the staircase to the lofted bed. Hooks swung down from behind the door. It was intricate without being fussy, clever without showing off.

Nothing was decorative. If something failed, the whole place would feel it.

She ran a hand along one of the joints last night, admiring the way it locked flush, almost invisible, until pressure gave it away. Whoever had designed Sophie had known how to use space like water in a bottle: no air wasted, every drop counted. It reminded her of Dr. Hill's voice—trim the thought until only the sharp edges stay.

She squirmed with a pleasantness she barely recognized, looking at her backpack where it sat square in Sophie's clever little loft.

A reliquary pared thin: extra socks, oats, her notebook and the fountain pen she still carried though it leaked, her college copy of Howard Zinn's *A People's History of the United States*. Tabs curling at the edges, every page scarred with fluorescent blue and yellow from a decade ago. It had settled into a nostalgic patina for Mara, and she'd even lost an hour flipping through its pages the night before, goosebumps rising at her younger handwriting.

Beside it, a softer relic: her paperback of DeLillo's *White Noise*, its cover sun-bleached, spine cracked. She wasn't sure why she'd packed it. Maybe because every line still sounded like a warning, like someone else had named the static in her chest years before she knew the word *panic*.

It made her imagine life at this scale. Just her backpack. A few pairs of clothes. A kettle, some oats, a book. Enough. How much simpler it might be, how much cleaner in her head, to have four walls that carried everything she needed and nothing she didn't.

A one-room life.

She'd sat by the fire ring with that thought circling last night, then locked herself inside, trying one of the novels from the shelf, checking and rechecking her phone: no bars. No Wi-Fi. None expected. None wanted. The absence scared her, and simplified her.

Each cabin came with a phone mounted by the door, rotary-style, 1960s Americana in a way that felt both kitsch and too much. Below it, a placard:

**Cabin Emergency Phone – Rings the Lodge Office Only.
No outside calls.**

The rotary dial unsettled her more than the lack of signal; it reminded her of her father's house.

By dark, she had given up on reading, and stared out the window instead. The view was ludicrous—snow draped across ground and pines, but alive with color, the green holding strong against winter.

At night, the woods glowed bright against the dark sky, the moonlight making it look like she was sleeping on a platform cantilevered into the forest.

Safe.

Alone.

Suspended in a dream.

Now, in daylight, she boiled water in the kettle and stirred oatmeal. Heat hummed from the vents along the floor. Toasty. Dry. She sat at the small table and thought of Dr. Hill. Of panic. Of exposure.

Years of SSRIs, therapy on and off, shifting diagnoses. *Panic disorder, proper,* Hill called it. His specialty. His creed: Panic is not illness, but wiring. An old survival system—screaming fire where no fire is. Avoidance was the trap. Fear of fear. The only way through was toward.

Acceptance.

Exposure.

Staying.

It echoed in her even here, as though her body were half waiting for the next alarm. Yet the cabin was quiet, steady, warm.

She dressed slowly, with a care that felt indulgent. The wool socks slid on thick and soft, perfect against the chill. Her boots laced tight with a sound she found satisfying, leather straining into place. Storm shell zipped, hood checked. Snow-rated bottoms layered over fleece leggings.

She'd spared no expense—except the gloves. A forgotten pair back in Michigan, lost to all her triple-checking. That failure needled her: She could count doors three times before leaving, but still forget what mattered.

Mara wore cheap gas-station mittens instead—thin red acrylic, already fuzzing at the seams. They would do. Most things did, if you understood their limits.

She locked the door with the code—2137—and stepped down the small bridge, gravel and snow crunching beneath her. It wasn't long before the bench she'd passed yesterday came into view. A trailhead sign she'd missed from the other angle was nailed to a tree. The rally point for the excursion.

It had snowed heavily but briefly in the night and stopped. This morning, the weather couldn't make up its mind. Not rain, not quite snow—just a thin, damp fall of half-formed flakes that melted on her sleeve but clung in the yellow-green grass.

The air felt weighted in a way that made her scalp prickle, as if the sky were waiting to choose its mood.

Darker patches of cloud drifted low, smudged and threatening, though for now the snow only sifted down in gentle flecks. Cold enough to bite, yet with that faint, deceptive hint of spring still riding under it—like the season hadn't fully decided which way to turn.

A thought struck, sudden and irrational: She could be stuck here forever if it stormed, her arrival swallowed before it even finished happening. No one would know. She told herself it was silly, but the thought clung like burrs.

If she'd booked a day earlier, the schedule would have handed her something almost quaint—an "edible and poisonous plants" hike, all talk of berries and bark and how not to die stupid. Or alternatively "primitive fire-making," the kind of survival-lite where you crouched over sticks until smoke curled up like applause. Harmless trials dressed up as wilderness skill.

But no—her slot had read Moonmilk Cavern. A

cave. Why that had sounded inviting, she couldn't say. Maybe because caves promised quiet, a cool place to stand still and breathe. Maybe because dark places carried their own gravity.

It wasn't just that. The activity meant a long ride, shared meals, awkward chatter with strangers—exposure, in every sense, pressing in as close as stone draperies overhead, with nowhere to step back.

And maybe that was the point. Dr. Hill, her therapist, said you don't pick what feels safe; you pick what feels impossible, and you choose to sit with it. That's how panic loses its teeth.

Maybe for other people a cave was a curiosity. A relaxing excursion. For her, it was work, and it was proof. If she could survive stone and strangers without coming apart, maybe she could survive herself.

Chapter 5

The tractor coughed to life at 9:30 on the dot, a steady diesel thrum that vibrated through the flatbed.

Mara hadn't expected to be here, wedged in with strangers, wrapped in scratchy wool. Only half an hour earlier she'd been standing at the rally point, shifting from boot to boot as the group assembled in a kind of uneasy orbit.

Introductions had been quick and shallow, more nods than words. Mara found herself cataloguing them the way she'd once catalogued classmates from the back of a lecture hall: posture, pairing, who orbited whom.

Two of them were obviously a couple—joined at the hip in that way people are when they've been weathered together. They had brought along a third, a woman who seemed to trail them like a satellite. She had the look of a friend folded into a trip that wasn't hers. Mara couldn't catch much of her face, but her posture gave her away: shoulders drawn, eyes cast low, deferential almost to the point of apology.

But it wasn't them Mara noticed most. It was the woman who had stepped out in front once the guide pointed them toward the trailhead. Brenna, the guide had called her. She carried herself with a kind of unconscious grace, boots crunching snow in a rhythm that set the pace for the rest of them.

Once, halfway down the path, she had turned back —just once—and their eyes had met. Amber and blue at the same time, searing and soothing in a way that made Mara's stomach fold in on itself. She'd looked away immediately, but the color of those eyes seemed to follow Mara, afterimage burn.

The six of them had walked maybe half a mile, following a narrow path through pines until it spilled into a clearing. There, waiting as if staged, sat a flatbed wagon fitted with rough benches and lumber rails. It was pulled by a tractor, and stacked on each bench were red-and-black wool blankets, folded neatly but clearly used, carrying the scent of hay and woodsmoke.

A gauze of moisture drifted down, more mist than snow or rain, clinging in fat drops to their jackets. The air seemed to hesitate, caught between thaw and freeze. But as Mara brushed her sleeve, she noticed the beads no longer ran slick—they crusted, hardened. The mist was losing its softness, tightening grain by grain into snow. Gore-Tex shells shed water quickly, rolling it off like mercury, but the cold snap edged in, turning each drop sharper.

The guide—apparently also the groundskeeper—had been talking as they filed in. He'd bent toward the only other man in the group, speaking low but not low enough to miss: something about "deer warts." A problem with the herd. Black swellings, strange growths. Mara's skin prickled at the words. She thought of the doe she'd seen the day before, her hide marred by pustules and tumorous bulges.

She half turned then, breath hitching, expecting to find those same prey eyes watching her from the tree line. But when she looked, nothing. Only woods and snow.

The feeling of eyes lingered anyway.

Now she braced herself as the wagon lurched forward, knees knocking the plank across from her. The driver-guide glanced back through the tractor's large rearview and lifted two fingers. Willy Thorne. Cap pulled low, gray threaded into his beard, posture of someone at home in the woods.

"What exactly is the Driftless?" Mara asked, pitching her voice over the engine as the wagon lurched forward.

Willy's eyes met hers in the mirror, a quick, pleased flash. "Geologists call it the Paleozoic Plateau," he said, letting the fancy term hang before he translated. "We call it Driftless because there's no glacial drift here—no gravel, no clay, no junk a glacier leaves behind. During the last ice age, the ice sheets flowed around this pocket like water around a rock. Never touched it."

"So it... skipped here?" Mara said.

"Split and went east and west," Willy said. The tractor eased onto a narrow track stitched between pines, the wagon swaying. "Everywhere else got scraped smooth. Here stayed rough. Old bones of the land right at the surface—sandstone, limestone. That's why you get the steep valleys—coulees—spring-fed creeks, caves." His voice took on a teacher's cadence, then softened. "I used to model this stuff for the Forest Service—groundwater, karst. A lot of screens and fluorescent lights." He looked away at the trees. "Turns out I like the outside part better."

She thought maybe panic was like this land: old wiring left behind, not erased by time. A pocket where fear still ruled, even if the rest of the world had smoothed it over.

"What's a coulee?" Mara asked, seizing on the word.

"Old French trapper word," Willy said, pleased again. "Means little valley. Here it's what rain and snowmelt carve when they get down into soft stone.

Steep sides, shady bottoms, streams that never run dry. Scars of water, not ice. Every coulee's its own pocket world."

They bumped over a frozen rut. The flatbed clattered; the hay bales creaked against their ropes. Five, maybe six miles an hour—slow on paper, fast when the wind kept reaching under your collar.

Willy pointed with two fingers, casual, sure. "Picture it—twenty thousand years ago. Mile-high ice out there," he said, tilting his chin toward the horizon. "But here? Open ground. Pockets of pine and oak holding on. A refuge. Everything alive in a circle of cold death."

Mara imagined it because he asked her to: this same ridge, no trail, no tractor, only wind and the groan of winter. A pocket of warmth, of water, in a world locked up. The thought landed behind her ribs.

"Moonmilk Cavern sits in limestone," Willy sputtered. "Dissolves easy. Water gets in, carves a lung out of the hill." He flicked another glance back. "Ever seen moonmilk before?"

"Moon what?"

"Looks delicate as frosting," he said, half a smile. "But it's rock. Calcite that grew like cream whipped stiff. If the air is still and the light hits right, it looks like the cave is breathing."

The track tilted. They climbed a shoulder of bluff, the valley opening on the left in layered grays: fields dappled with snow, dark ribbons of creek, the far line of trees like charcoal. The tractor's rear tires were as tall as Mara's chest, cleated with mud and frost. A utility rig, not a field tractor—quieter, tighter, built to haul instead of thunder. It moved with a patient inevitability, putting miles under them one judder at a time.

"How far is the cave?" she asked.

"Depends on the conditions and the route we take," Willy said. "Plan is for two hours out, same back. Plenty of daylight." He checked his watch like a habit he hadn't shaken, though out here, time belonged more to weather than to hours. For the briefest second his eyes flicked east—expression shuttered—then back to the trail. "We'll stop for lunch midway, then warm up again at the cave entrance. Coffee, maybe a little fire if the wind lets us."

He didn't grandstand. He just talked—naming the cuts they rattled through, pointing out a spring where ice formed in plates instead of sheets. Book-smart words when they fit—"loess," "karst," "coulee"—plain words when they mattered. The kind of voice you'd follow into the woods without thinking to ask why.

Across from her sat Carl and Carly Fenwick, matching green eyes, close enough in posture that Mara could feel the warmth between them. Mature, handsome in that lived-in way, dressed in brands that looked high-class but carried without flash.

Carly wore a bright blue wool cap pulled low, its

edge brushing Carl's shoulder whenever the wagon lurched.

Their gear was clean, coordinated, expensive in the way people who no longer worried about budgets bought things—without thinking twice. Their kindness showed in how they listened—heads tilted, smiles catching not at their own words but at another's.

Beside them sat Gwen Caddell, quieter, her occasional reactions folding into theirs with the ease of long familiarity. When the tractor jolted, Gwen flinched as if she'd done something wrong, then folded her hands tighter in her lap. Mara noticed her eyes. Gwen's were glassy-dark, like wells—deep, knowing. Not ordinary. But not beautiful.

These three seemed bound, but unevenly: two woven tight, the third trailing. Gwen's place felt conditional—present out of duty or habit more than affection. It was a structure that worked only if everyone stayed in their place.

Mara noticed how often Gwen's eyes flicked to the others, not in search of praise but to keep her bearings. Where they stood, she stood. What they touched, she touched.

Carl didn't seem to notice Gwen at all, his gaze sliding past as though she were furniture. Carly did notice, though—returned her glances with a faint, distracted tenderness, the kind of care one might show a younger sister. It almost looked natural, but it wasn't affection.

Then there was Brenna. Her eyes had depth, but not the fragile kind. These were eyes that had learned to endure—honed by aggression, calculation, and a quiet, predatory patience. When they met Mara's, the intensity felt almost animal, refined to pursuit and capture. The burn of her gaze left Mara's chest hollow, breath punched out and slow to return.

What or who Brenna might have hunted, Mara couldn't say. But she knew this much: She'd never seen eyes like that before. They unsettled her, made her pulse quicken, yet she found herself leaning toward them all the same. For better or worse, you couldn't slip past Brenna unseen.

And Mara—consequences be damned—wanted nothing more than to be seen by Brenna.

Chapter 6

Carl startled them all when he shouted, half standing, arm stabbing toward the trees. "There—look!"

The wagon jostled with his movement, everyone's eyes dragged to the spot. A forestry marker leaned at an angle in the snow, its wood pale with weather. The faded paint showed the old cave symbol: a curved arch, shadow stroke beneath, an arrow etched beside it. A relic pointing into the woods.

Mara squinted. Whatever words had once spelled the route had long been scoured away. The spur looked corrupted—fresh snow lay smooth, unbroken across its mouth, as if the forest itself had closed it off. By contrast, the main track beneath them showed pressed lines of hooves and tires, rutted but steady, alive with use.

Willy caught Carl's eye in the rearview. His voice

dropped, low enough that the engine almost ate it. "Shorter by miles. But we don't use that one."

Carl frowned. "Why not?" He smoothed a cuff, and the tiniest head tilt—half eye-roll, half blink—flashed and vanished, polite as a reflex.

"Equestrian riders. Snowmobiles. Dirt bikes too," Willy said. His jaw worked as if grinding down something unsaid. "Couple of boys came through once. Brothers. Young, fast, too fast. Someone had strung wire across the trail. Thin. Strong."

The wagon itself seemed to creak louder, as if listening.

Willy lifted his hand, brushed his shoulder without thinking. "The older one hit. Caught him here. Flipped him. Broke him up bad, but he lived."

Carl leaned forward, voice rasping. "And the other?"

Willy didn't answer. His gaze lingered on the spur, eyes caught in its snare. At last his bare fingers went higher, to his throat. He left them there. The silence stretched until the answer was obvious.

Carl's face twitched, refusing the implication. "You mean his head came off?"

"I mean he didn't make it," Willy said flat. His eyes stayed forward. His thumb worried the brim of his cap, pressing the fabric like he needed something steady under his hand.

Mara's stomach tightened. She had read about that

kind of thing—fatal pranks, wires strung between trees where kids tore through on bikes. Invisible until it caught you at the chest or throat. She remembered cases: one in Michigan, another maybe Oregon. Helmets no defense, bodies flung, boys who had thought they were flying until they weren't. The thought stuck: how malice could wait in the trees like an animal, patient, invisible.

Carly shifted, unease breaking her silence. "How long ago was this?" Her voice was soft but pointed, a careful question looking for truth.

"Years," Willy said—too quick, like a door slammed.

"Did you see it?" she pressed, gentler, not prying so much as trying to set something right in her head.

His jaw tightened. No answer.

Carl shook his head once—small, practiced, the social kind of dismissal you could deny later—and looked back to the main track as if efficiency itself should settle the matter. "And after all this time, you still won't use the shorter way?"

The silence this time felt different—dense, as though the trees themselves bent in to listen.

Finally, Willy said, "After that... other things happened."

No one spoke. The pines flickered light and shadow across his face as he went on.

Brenna's mouth lifted at one corner—a brief, unreadable smirk—as though she were measuring Willy, not the story.

The wagon rattled, hushed except for the growl of the engine.

After a long minute, Willy spoke again, quieter. "Snowmobiler. They found him face-down in the creek by the spur. Water iced halfway over his back. Helmet still strapped on. Machine wasn't wrecked—it was upright on the bank. Engine off. Full tank. Key still in."

His jaw worked, eyes fixed straight ahead. "Looked like he'd stepped off, laid himself down in the water. But not like drowning, either. Lungs were clear. No ice, no water. Coroner wrote heart failure. Exposure. Things you write down when you don't have better words." He hesitated, voice thinning. "But people who saw him said it looked different. Like he'd pushed his head under, held it there, and just... stopped."

He let out a breath, almost a sigh. "Bad ground. Things don't end right there. Not a good route."

The air itself had changed. The damp, misty weight of earlier was gone, replaced by brittle dryness that bit her lips when she breathed. The storm had chosen its side. What fell now wasn't soft snow but sharp flakes, dry as ash, skittering sideways. They didn't cling—they struck. Tiny needles hissed against the boards, tapped Mara's cheek like static.

The wagon rocked on. No one argued. They passed

until the marker seemed to vanish behind them, less a guidepost, Mara thought, than a grave.

It wasn't fear that kept people off that spur, she realized. It was memory.

Silence stretched. Willy's voice returned, steadier now, almost as if he felt the quiet grow too thick. "Think of it—dark sky, fire's a coin of light in your hands. Everything you need inside that circle." He paused, just long enough for the cold to fill the gap. "Everything that wants you is outside it."

It took Mara a moment to realize he was talking about the Driftless again. About this place, this odd pocket of land that ice had spared.

She looked around as the wagon jolted forward. Cold now, decisively; the air prickled her skin as though the past still breathed here and liked the taste of her. She imagined it long ago—the same ridge hemmed in by walls of ice so high they erased the horizon.

The Driftless.

A refuge, yes, but also a trap—life encircled by death. Willy's words had settled, weighty.

The wagon pitched over a rut hard.

Mara's chest lit like a struck match—a flare of panic before she even knew it. Her body did the old trick: heart climbing, throat prickling, breath clipping short, nerves firing in hot, stupid bursts. Fear forming.

She pulled the blanket tighter, forcing herself to ride

it. The buzz stayed caged in her ribs, vibrating like an insect that wanted out. This was the loop. Trigger, fear, symptoms, more fear.

Fear of fear.

Dr. Hill had explained it a dozen times: Panic was a false alarm system, a smoke detector blaring over burnt toast. Still, her brain argued louder—what if it isn't false this time? What if I pass out right here? What if my body really quits?

Her chest squeezed harder.

Or worse—what if I snap? What if I stand, jump off, make a scene? Her hands twitched, her stomach turned. She imagined herself crumpling, or being hauled back to camp, everyone watching, pitying. Shame layered on top of panic until she wanted to sob just from the weight of it.

She recognized it even as it happened. Catastrophic thinking. Safety behaviors. Anticipatory anxiety. All the terms lived in her head like index cards, but knowing didn't stop the body. Her pulse still raced, her breath still stuck in her throat.

Dr. Hill's voice came back, practiced and calm, as though stitched into her: Sit with it. Let it be a tremor, not a sentence. Let it crest and fall. She shaped the words in her mind, mantra-like: *I'm having the thought that this is danger. I'm choosing to ride it out. Naming it as thought, not fact.*

Words weren't lethal.

She gripped the blanket until her knuckles hurt. *This is adrenaline. This is my amygdala screaming tiger when it's just snow and strangers. It will pass.*

Saying it that way almost let her believe it.

And then—predictably, yet somehow to her own surprise—it did pass. Within minutes she found herself not panicking, not jumping from a moving vehicle, not passing out in front of a trailer full of strangers.

Instead, she was sitting upright, breath steadying, heart loosening its grip. To her faint astonishment, she even caught herself passing for normal—laughing at the right moments, nodding when others spoke.

For all anyone knew, she was doing well.

Her eyes caught Carly's for a moment, a half smile offered across the bench—concern behind it, not pity, a question she wasn't quite asking. It landed like a weight Mara wasn't ready to carry. She turned away. Safer that way. Still—the fact lingered. She was fitting in.

Her gaze skimmed Gwen. Silent, pretty in a subdued way. A face designed to endure quietly. Not magnetic. Gwen's eyes were still a touch too wide.

And then Brenna. Brenna's irises shifted amber-blue, catching the snowlight, alive even in shadow. The corner of her mouth held that faint, private smirk, as if she'd clocked every pulse in the wagon and didn't mind.

Mara hated how those eyes tethered her. How her chest tightened at the sight.

Willy's words about refuge and coulees drifted back on the cold air. The language of survival. Mara thought: *Maybe that's me.* A pocket of warmth ringed by glaciers. Still alive. Still here. Not smooth, not scraped flat.

Old bones showing through.

A survivor.

She forced herself to practice: watching the Fenwicks, Gwen, Brenna. Nodding when they laughed. Arranging her face in the shape of interest. Dr. Hill had called it a skill, not a lie—half of social life was teaching your body the shape of belonging, even if words stayed stuck. Still, her throat worked against her, stubborn as ever, when conversation threatened to reach her.

The wagon rattled forward through snow and silence. Shadows knit tighter overhead. Around her, the group shifted, murmured, watched the trees.

And all of it—the grave-marker trail, the bad ground, the haunted air—felt like the woods had stopped watching them and started judging.

Chapter 7

Cold gnawed through the blanket on Mara's lap, and her butt had gone from sore to numb to sore again. She finally folded the blanket twice and sat on it instead. Relief. Carly noticed, smiled faintly, and did the same; Brenna followed without a word.

Carl stayed put, broad-shouldered and steady, until his voice cut through the engine thrum: "Willy—you said lunch and fire midway, right? We've been going near ninety minutes."

The question hung heavier than it should have. Mara realized she hadn't heard Willy in a while. He'd been naming ridges, pointing out springs, speaking in that steady cadence—but then... nothing.

She looked now.

Willy's eyes were turned east, his expression unsettled. He flicked a quick glance at his watch, thumb brushing the glass like he was cleaning it, then raised his voice too brightly: "Didn't like the weather, so I pushed us along a bit further. Food and warmth soon."

The tractor jolted to a stop, hard enough to rattle bone against wood. Pain shot through Mara's backside, but the stillness was worse—cold closed in, sharper for some reason now that the wagon no longer carried them forward.

Willy swung down. He hauled out a bundle of split wood bound with a fabric strip, tossed it down, then produced a small white block no larger than a bar of soap, a stub of twine jutting from its center. His eyes caught Mara's for a beat—steady, unreadable—before he nodded toward a patch of yellow grass where the snow thinned.

He worked with unhurried precision, scuffing away needles and snow until soil showed. The wood stacked into a loose pyramid, space left for air. The "soap" caught instantly when he touched it with a lit match, dripping molten fire into the kindling until it snapped alive. A fire starter, Mara realized. She'd nearly washed her hands with one back at Sophie.

"Hands," he said, glancing at her red knuckles. He mimed a motion. "Don't thrust them in—cup above the flame, let the heat climb. Warms the blood, not the skin."

She mirrored him. The heat rose like a living thing

and slipped under her palms; it hurt, then fed her. Willy watched once, then looked back to the wood, satisfied.

Five minutes—no more—and the fire was awake: a crackling body of orange heat pushing back the February bite.

The sound of the world changed; the engine hush drifted away and the woods took on that Christmas quiet, every limb frosted, every noise padded. They circled the fire instinctively, six shapes leaning toward it like iron filings to a magnet.

A coin of light in their hands, Willy had called it earlier. Everything you needed inside that circle. A thought pressed in on Mara: Circles only held if everyone stayed.

The fire recast them. Carl's face looked boyish in the sparks. Carly's mouth softened into something unguarded. Gwen's silence read as wary, not aloof; she grimaced at the heat's first bite and then smoothed her expression flat, as if even discomfort should be polite. Brenna's eyes caught the light like molten gold. And Willy—ember-lit, lines deepened, like someone carved from the land itself.

Mara slipped off her cheap mittens, holding her hands out the way he'd shown.

The dense snow drifted in flakes big as feathers, settling on sleeves and hair before surrendering to the glow. She felt the warmth in her chest, like some ancient hunger being met.

Dr. Hill's voice drifted up: fire as survival, fire as companion. One flame carried to another across ice and hunger. And now—six souls in a Wisconsin wood, faces caught in the same old light.

Willy dusted his hands. "Any vegetarians here?" No one moved. His shoulders eased. "Good. The veggie can tastes like punishment." A flash of dry humor, gone quick.

He set down five unmarked cans, stamped only with dates and three black letters: BBB. He pierced them with quick, precise motions—tap, pop, tap, pop—five cans opened clean. Exact. A rhythm born of countless repetitions. Something in it bordered on ritual.

"Here," he said to Mara without fuss, producing a pair of wool liners from his jacket pocket—spares, darker at the palms from honest use. "Wear these under your... situation." His mouth tilted at her gas-station mittens; not unkind.

"Thank you," she said, and meant it more than felt reasonable. She slid them on. Heat stayed this time, didn't leak.

He rested the cans at the fire's edge, flames licking their sides. The vents hissed faint steam. The smell rose quickly—beans, bacon, beef—fatty and rich, tugging at Mara's throat.

"BBB," she murmured under her breath. Bean, bacon, beef.

He caught her gaze just long enough to make her think he'd heard, then gave a small smile. "Get comfortable. This part takes care of itself."

He unscrewed a black-lidded jar. Inside: white, whipped, like butter left too long in the churn. With a wooden spork he scooped spoonfuls into each can. The broth deepened instantly—meat turned velvet, beans sinking into something darker, richer.

"It's beans, bacon, beef," he said simply. "And what I added was tallow."

"Oh my god," Brenna breathed. Her voice was softer than Mara expected—higher, almost musical. The first words she'd spoken since introductions. Five words total, and Mara already wanted more. Another private smirk tugged one corner of Brenna's mouth, there and gone, like she'd caught Willy out in a luxury disguised as roughing it.

Carly's fork hovered. "What's tallow?" she asked, curious, not squeamish.

"Rendered beef fat," Willy said, easy. "Doesn't sound pretty, but it keeps. Adds depth. Old camp trick."

Gwen's nose wrinkled before she flattened it away, ladylike. "Mm," she said, as if agreement could smooth taste.

Carly hesitated, then ate. Her face loosened with

relief. Carl gave her knee a gentle squeeze, pride quick and neat—the practiced intimacy of a couple that knew how to perform ease. When Willy glanced east again, Carl's eyes flicked there too, then back with the lightest head shake—tidy skepticism you could miss if you weren't looking.

Mara bent over her own can, grateful no one was watching. The beans carried smoke, the bacon salt, the beef body—and the tallow tied it all together, coating her tongue, warmth spreading deeper than food alone. She ate like someone starved, and in a way, she was. Not of calories but of steadiness, of moments that made her body believe it could endure.

"Good fire," she murmured.

"Good company," Willy said, and poked a coal into place, the smallest compliment returned like he was straightening a picture frame.

Snow came thicker, muffling everything, flakes fat and slow. The circle lingered, silence broken only by the gentle rasp of wood against tin, a hollow clink softened by grain. Not the harsh scrape of metal, but something quieter—rounded, almost intimate, like the sound of a spoon stirring broth by firelight.

For a while, Mara's shoulders forgot tension. She watched Willy watch the sky—the habit of a man who could enjoy a fire and still count clouds.

When he doused the flames, the smoke didn't tear

away; it folded, sank, then drifted sideways in one sheet, as if the snow were a lung exhaling. Willy followed it with his eyes. "Wind's changing," he said to no one in particular. "We'll want to be moving."

Carl brushed snow from his coat. "So tell me, Willy—ever been anyone else who didn't make it out of here?" Too casual to be curiosity.

Willy shrugged. "Woods'll take what they want." He said it lightly, but he clicked the jar tight and stowed it like a man who'd learned to put things away before the weather decided for him.

They climbed back into the wagon. The benches weren't softer, but Mara wrapped her blanket around her shoulders instead of under her thighs. Brenna did the same, steam rising faintly from her sleeves.

Mara felt good—warm despite the cold. Not relaxed, not really, but brushing close to it.

She went back to one of her tricks: ask, don't answer. People loved to talk about themselves. A simple question could buy her minutes. Open-ended was safest—*how* over *why*. When she blanked, there were always the easy anchors: family, travel, food. Things that spun without ever circling back to her.

She tried one. "How long have you two been married?"

Carly tilted a smile. "At the beginning..." Not an answer, exactly. But definitely the start of one.

Mara nodded like she understood and cared as Carly babbled on about her coupling with Carl. Another trick: nod, then let the silence work. Most people rushed to fill it. It kept the focus off her, made her look—hopefully—like a good listener.

Sometimes she made a game of it. How long could she go without speaking and still seem engaged? She'd learned to laugh a beat after everyone else, tilt her head just enough to suggest she was following. Exhausting, yes. But it worked.

The tractor groaned forward. The wagon swayed. Mara glanced at Willy. He wasn't listening. His gaze had gone past them again, to the white—no horizon now, just space erasing itself.

The big flakes that had hushed the world began to stack into ridges; the hush grew heavier, a quiet that made every breath sound private. Wind shouldered through, tugging at hoods and seams. The puffy drifts they'd eaten lunch beneath slumped and slid, then froze to cornices along the track.

Willy's jaw worked, concern leaving a faint track across his features, like a sled line in new snow. Mara felt her chest answer, the old buzz waking as if his worry tuned her body like a string.

The storm wasn't here yet. But it had found its edge, and it had started cutting—soft, deep, everywhere at once.

Chapter 8

The wagon had just begun to tilt downhill, pace quickening—not fast, maybe ten miles an hour, but enough that the wind felt sharpened against her face.

Then the world cracked.

It wasn't wood splitting or ice breaking—it was skull against skull, marrow-deep, a blow that rang through Mara's jaw and bladder like she'd crested a hill too fast while bumping her head hard. The kind of pain that made you clench, praying not to piss yourself.

Her body snapped forward, then sideways, weightless for a beat—a falling sensation before she understood that she wasn't in the wagon anymore.

And then—nothing. Snow and dirt pressed against her cheek. She was on the ground—cold packed against her face, breath fogging sideways.

For a moment, maybe two, she couldn't see. Sight gone, black as if her eyelids were welded shut. *Am I blind? Am I dead? I can't see—I can't see—* Panic licked sharp: blind, struck, broken. The thought stampeded— *What if it doesn't come back? What if this is it?*

Then vision seeped in, a smeared blur, light and shape leaking through fog.

When it cleared enough to mean something, she realized she was lying in churned snow. To her right, ten feet away, the top of the flatbed loomed sideways, facing her like a wall.

The wagon had flipped on its side.

The tractor that pulled it was gone.

She pushed herself up slightly on shaky elbows. That's when she saw it: Twenty yards ahead, the tractor nosed into a ditch, its left rear tire hanging uselessly in the air.

The air reeked: hot diesel, raw soil, and something sweet but spoiled, sharp enough to sting her throat. Smoke curled low, thin as gauze. Somewhere inside the ruined machine a piece of metal ticked and cooled, an idle, metallic heartbeat nearing flatline.

Mara forced herself upright from her elbows, half standing at first, the world tilting black at the edges, knees trembling, but she locked them anyway and refused to fall.

The air was too quiet. No engine, no wheels, no

Willy's steady voice. Just the tick of hot metal and her own ragged breath.

Then other sounds bled in—a low moan, wet and pained. Cloth dragging on snow. A cough that snapped into silence.

Her head whipped, vision still swimming, but her ears worked fine. There were six of them, six bodies. *Where are they?*

To her left: a shape hunched and trembling, shoulders jerking. Gwen? Or Carly? Hard to tell through the blur.

Behind her: a high, wheezing breath, sharp little bursts that made her own chest tighten in sympathy. Brenna. Small lungs, small body, sound too fragile.

She forced herself to focus. Hypervigilance wrapped around her, dragging her through the fog. Every smell, every sound, every detail had to mean something. The sweetness in the air wasn't only fuel. Blood had sugar too.

Mara's voice cracked out: "Hey!"

No one answered.

Only the wagon creaked where it lay on its side, and the faint hiss of smoke that sounded far too much like breathing.

A shadow moved through the blur—steady, upright. Willy. He strode into the wreckage without hurry, voice pitched loud enough to cut the groans but still unnervingly calm. He moved like someone who had already decided what mattered.

"Who's hurt?"

Not if. Who.

Carl sat braced against the overturned wagon, his face pale, clutching his left hand with his right like he could hold the pain in. His jaw tightened as he grimaced. "It's fine," he muttered through his teeth, though his eyes said otherwise.

She saw Brenna—limping slightly, one arm held close, blood matted at her ear and threaded through her hair. Mara's gaze went straight to her eyes. Clear. Untouched. The relief that hit her was fierce and embarrassing, as if something essential had been spared.

Carly wasn't fine.

Mara's stomach turned at the sight: one finger bent at an impossible angle, twisted and clearly broken, pointing as if accusing her own wrist. Worse was her arm—a foot-long swath of skin flayed back, raw and wet. Not a cut but a peeled layer—flesh beading blood in tiny porous dots, seeping.

The blood against the snow around them was obscene—crimson blooming across white like ink in paper. It shocked her how perfect whiteness could be ruined with one spreading blot.

Carly didn't even see it. She sat on the ground slack, staring past them all into the trees as if she'd missed her own body. Shock hollowed her face. It wasn't until Carl swore, voice snapping sharp, that her gaze dropped to her arm.

The scream came then—shrill, piercing, too human—and she clutched the ruined appendage only to shriek louder at the contact.

Mara hadn't thought the scene could get worse, but watching Carly unravel like that cracked something in her. The wail hit harder than the blood. Her own breath broke, and before she realized it, her legs had given way. She dropped to her knees on the packed snow with a dull thump, a sob coming loose from her throat, sharp and humiliating.

What are we doing here? The thought tore through her like teeth. *What if it were me? What if I pass out right now, or break a leg, or worse? How do we even get back? Why did I come?* Each question fed the next until her body shook, panic looping fast, feeding itself like fire swallowing its own smoke.

Her vision tunneled and left again, breath scraping short. She went to her knees again, pressed her palms flat into the snow, the burn of cold biting through her skin, forcing herself to hold on to something real.

Still here. Still breathing. Still here. She tried to make the words land, a mantra barely audible under the ringing of Carly's howl.

Gradually, shapes returned again—blurred figures

moving in the churn of snow, cries overlapping with the hiss of wind. Her focus staggered from Carly's wrecked arm to the others.

Gwen had fared better, though "better" was generous. A deep gash slashed across one cheek, bright against her pale skin. Blood traced down from her opposite eyebrow, a grotesque symmetry. "Oh my god," she muttered before her eyes widened and she pressed her lips tight, ashamed at the slip.

Willy crouched by his pack and came up with a roll of gauze—small, civilian, laughably insufficient for the damaged bodies around them. He tore at it fast, steady hands working with Carl's, both of them locking in on Carly.

They wrapped her arm first. The gauze vanished against the raw length of skin, white already blotched red, then redder. By the time Willy finished winding, dark color was already pushing through the weave in slow blooms. Not enough material to matter much. Not against that kind of wound.

Her hand came next. Willy braced her wrist while Carl wound the last strip, forcing her broken finger into the binding. Another wail. Mara had to look away when the bone seemed to point sideways through the layers, warped and obscene, the gauze tugging tight around it like a shroud.

That was it. Roll empty. Willy didn't hesitate—he

stripped off his coat and pressed it into Carl's hands. Together they wrapped it over the sodden gauze, tying it into a bulky splint of sorts. Carly's face stayed strangely calm through the rest of the work, lips pressed flat, eyes glassy, as if she were already somewhere else. But every so often, a tiny sound slipped out—a whimper, sharp and high, betraying her body no matter what her mind tried to mask.

Mara saw Willy's bloodied hands and then her own—her fingers smeared red. She reached to the back of her head and found heat, then pain. When she looked again, her skin was stained, the red unmistakably hers.

Her right knee throbbed strangely too. Not sharp pain yet, but wrong—as if the hinge had slipped inside the joint. She shifted her weight, testing it. It held, for now.

Something inside her wanted to act.

Humans help humans, she thought.

Mara fumbled at her hands, tugging off the spare wool liners Willy had lent her. She pressed them into Carly's good palm, leaving herself with only the thin gas-station mittens. Willy glanced at her, then gave a single nod—just approval. Enough.

The silence between screams was worse.

The storm's snow pressed close, muffling sound until even cries seemed swallowed.

Brenna's voice cut in then, sharp and cool: "How far to the cave?"

Willy didn't answer. He only looked at her once, a quick flash of disbelief, then back to Carly's wound. His face said the question was ridiculous. He didn't have time for it, not now.

The others clustered around Carly, Carl's jaw tight, Gwen's sleeve pressed to the wound on her own cheek. Willy gave the last knot in the coat wrap a final tug, his hands streaked with her blood. He exhaled once, long, then looked up at them all.

Then Carl snapped, voice ragged with fury, the disdain curling even in pain: "How the hell do you crash us like that? You've driven this trail a hundred times—how do you bury a tractor, Willy?"

Willy's eyes lifted, calm and hard as flint. His voice came back like a door slamming shut.

"This wasn't an accident."

The words landed in the muffled hush, snow drinking the sound, but the meaning burned through like fire on ice.

Chapter 9

They moved in stutters, less a group than a scatter of broken parts nudged toward the same point.

Willy's words still rang in Mara's skull—*this wasn't an accident*—and now he walked like he was following evidence, not wreckage.

His hand cut the air once, steady and unyielding, gesturing them toward the ditch ahead where the tractor lay collapsed like something slaughtered.

The wreck spoke in fragments. Metal pinged as it cooled, each tick sharp in the brittle air. A hiss of diesel leaked somewhere unseen, weaving with the copper-sweet tang of blood until the woods themselves smelled spoiled. Smoke curled low over the snow, thin and acrid.

The quiet that followed was not empty but crowded—broken breaths, fabric dragging, a wet cough cut off quick. Somewhere close, a branch gave under ice and snapped, the report so sudden it jolted Mara's chest. Then only the creak of the ruined wagon, rocking faintly as if the forest wind was testing its weight.

Willy's mouth moved, his arm slicing the air, but to Mara it was only steam in her ears—a kettle shrieking, the world reduced to noise. For half a breath she thought she caught a word—*move*—before it dissolved back into static.

Not blind. Not deaf. Just stunned. She blinked and forced herself to focus on the people around her.

Gwen staggered past, clutching the small of her back as if a hidden knife twisted there. Her face was pale, one cheek gashed open, but what drew Mara's eye was higher—the left side of her scalp torn in a strip. Not deep, but grotesque, a bolt or screw had carved the skin away like a zipper ripped open. The flap clung in her hair, sticky and raw, as though the woods had tried to peel her. Gwen winced when she brushed it, fingers trembling, then dropped her hand quickly as if not wanting to know.

Behind them, Carl wrestled Carly upright. She swayed on her feet, the ruined arm bound in Willy's coat. Now Mara saw more: a rip at her thigh, snow pants cut open and cinched back together with clumsy hands, fabric bulging where Carl had tied a strip of his own shirt tight beneath.

The outer tear looked laughably small—no more than a puncture, a hole punched in cloth. But when Carly shifted, when her boot dragged across the snow, red unfurled from where she'd been sitting. Blood bled into the perfect white, blooming outward like ink on blotting paper.

Carl hissed at the sight, then caught it back in his throat. He tried to adjust her without showing the effort, but the motion betrayed him. His own wrist jerked awkwardly, and he made a strangled whimper, face pinched as if the sound had escaped without permission. Still he hauled his wife, jaw tight, forcing steadiness he didn't have.

Gwen drifted closer then. She looked at her sister Carly, at Carl, with something stripped of pride—not pity, not even comfort, but the desperate need to be near another body. Her arms twitched half open, an instinctive reach for contact, for witness. For a heartbeat, Mara thought Carl might let her. Thought they might all collapse together in the snow, some crooked knot of family warmth.

But Carl never turned. Without looking, he half shoved her with his shoulder. It was subtle, deniable, but Mara saw it. His face cut toward Carly instead, gaze fixed sharp on her as if the others had ceased to exist.

And Carly—pale, blood soaking into snow beneath her boots—managed a glance at Gwen, a flash of irritation, then a brief hiss sharp enough it bared her teeth. Not words, not really a sound at all. Just possession. Fury that Gwen had tried to breach something that wasn't hers.

Mara saw it land. Saw Gwen flinch as if slapped, her lip trembling once before she bit it flat. Mara's hand even lifted, half reaching, wanting to steady her, to close the space Carl had opened. But Gwen turned before she could, shoulders hunched, falling in behind the pair like a shadow relegated to its proper distance.

It left a heat in Mara's chest. Anger, sharp. Not at Carl, not at Carly, but at Gwen herself. For yielding. For folding when she should have stood.

And then her own body reminded her to focus on herself: the knee, loose inside as if some gear had slipped a tooth. Every step felt like a dare, the joint threatening to crumble sideways with no warning, sharp little edges biting when she shifted wrong.

Her head throbbed differently—not just ache, but a wet pressure, as if something had been poured between her skull and scalp and was sloshing there, every heartbeat a pulse that wanted out. Sometimes it swelled into a white flash behind her eyes, and she had to blink to be sure the world was still real.

Snow had thickened too, soft now, falling heavy and slow. It muffled the woods, dulled the broken breaths and dragging feet, so that Mara couldn't tell what the storm swallowed and what her own ears failed to hold.

Where was Brenna?

The thought bit through her, and then she saw—Brenna already at the edge of the ditch beside Willy, slight frame upright, a bloody ear matted dark against her hair. The red streak ran thick down her neck, pooling at the collar of her jacket. Skin abrasions there too, raw, the promise of blooming bruises by nightfall. But what stopped Mara wasn't the blood.

It was the stare.

Brenna's eyes fixed straight on her, unblinking. Not dazed. Not lost. Suspicious. Skeptical in a way no words had shaped yet but clear all the same—as if she'd caught Mara in some motion unseen, some slip in her face or voice. The girl didn't speak, didn't point. She only looked, and the look said enough: *I noticed. I don't like what I noticed.*

Mara's stomach clenched, but she met the gaze and held it. Too long. Until Willy shifted and Brenna broke off, turning back to the ditch. The interruption left Mara oddly shaken—as if her need to be seen, to be liked by Brenna of all people, had been laid bare and then abruptly snatched away.

Willy's voice reached them then. She saw his mouth move, saw his arm point toward the ditch again, but her ears only gave her a whistle, a flattening scream inside her head. Still, the cut of his hand through the air steadied her, a signal clear enough even when sound had failed.

She turned to Carl. His eyes caught her.

The right one, red and watering, a burst of vessels feathering through the white. But it was the other that held her—bloodshot to the rim, the iris drowned by a dark spreading blot, as though ink had pooled there and refused to clear. The lid above it was puffing, swelling visibly even as she stared. The effect was grotesque. A face half familiar, half wrecked, human made strange.

Mara looked away fast, breath caught.

And in that stolen glance she saw Brenna again, a step behind now, steadying Gwen with a hand at her elbow. No hardness in her face now, no suspicion—only a quick, instinctive touch, the kind someone gives without thinking. Concern, plain and unguarded.

Mara felt the surprise tighten her chest. Even Brenna—the one who seemed sharpest, least forgiving—cared enough to reach out for another human. She wished it had been her.

It unsettled her more than Carl's eyes or Carly's hiss. For a moment, Brenna's concern carried something Mara hadn't expected to last in this wreck of bodies: Even here, someone still thought to hold a stranger upright.

They were moving, she realized. Forward, together,

all of them staggering toward the shape of the tractor in the snow. Not survivors, not yet. Just wounded animals following the hand of the one who still walked straight.

Mara's knee buckled once, nearly spilling her, and she caught herself against air. Her head swam with wet heat, each heartbeat a hammer tapping at the wound beneath her hair.

She glanced sidelong again—at Carly's teeth clenched hard enough they might crack, at Gwen pressing her scalp now with a shaking hand, at Brenna still anchoring as she steadied someone else. Broken, all of them, yet still upright.

The ditch loomed closer, the wrecked tractor crouched like a carcass. Diesel fumes mingled with pine resin, cloying, inescapable. Willy's figure stood there already, dark and straight, as if he'd been waiting for them.

And maybe for this.

Chapter 10

The ditch yawned ahead—three feet deep, wide enough to swallow the tractor's front end. Its edges were clean, squared, raw. Not erosion. Dug.

Willy stood at the lip of it, boots planted where the tractor had come to a dead stop. "The wagon went first," he said, pointing back down the trail. Snow had drifted just enough to reveal a second cut they'd missed before— a trench carved lengthwise along the inside edge of the trail. Clean, straight edges like the one that ate the tractor. "Right there. Weight shifted wrong, and it rolled the wagon."

He gestured forward again, toward the deeper pit where the tractor's nose had buried itself. "I had enough momentum I couldn't stop. It was over before I knew what was happening."

Mara looked from the tractor back to the trail, breath fogging, forcing the ground to assemble itself in her head.

And then she saw it.

The trench that flipped them was long and narrow, running with the trail like a channel—covered in places with branches, skimmed with fresh snow. Concealed.

Like an inverted L.

Once she saw it, the crash replayed with sickening clarity: The inside wheel dropped into it at the bend—like a rail—and the wagon's weight pitched over the trapped side. Then, with no time to correct, the tractor's momentum fed it straight into the pit ahead.

"That's not all of it," Willy said.

He crouched and brushed snow aside with a bare hand. Metal winked back —dull, gray, ugly. A steel cable, thick and barbed, laid low and angled beneath the skim of snow. It had cinched around the tractor's undercarriage and the inside of the right wheel, like a snare.

Not strung high.

Not meant to clothesline.

Meant to hook.

Meant to hold.

"The cable caught underneath," Willy said. "Once it cinched—"

"Christ," Carl muttered. His voice was low, but his face betrayed more—the quick flex of his jaw, the sideways twitch of his eyes. Mara had already noticed the man's gift for disdain: small, deniable tells that cut deeper than words.

Willy stayed crouched, his hand still resting on the cable. He dragged his boot along the edge of the pit, exposing the soil beneath.

The cut was too clean, too even.

"This wasn't dug with a shovel," he said. He glanced along the trench's length, eyes narrowing. "This took equipment. Backhoe, maybe. Someone took time shaping it. Hiding it."

Silence pooled around them.

Gwen swallowed. "So... someone did this on purpose."

No one answered her at first.

Willy nodded once.

Gwen's voice thinned. "To what—scare us?"

Willy didn't answer right away. He stayed crouched, fingers still on the cable as if he could feel the intention humming through it.

"You don't do this to scare people," he said at last. "And they did it recently." He looked up, eyes hard. "Someone knew we'd be here."

No one spoke. The only sound was Carly's small shift under Carl's coat. Her mouth moved like she might speak, but nothing came out.

"The cave," Brenna said. "If it's close—warmth, power, help."

Carl latched on. "Yeah. Let's just follow the trail on foot past this shit."

Willy turned. One flat look.

Willy didn't look back at the ditch. His gaze was now fixed on the trail ahead, jaw working once before he spoke.

"We need to get off this route," he said. Not loud. Not panicked. But something in his voice had gone tight, compressed, as if he were packing more into the words than he meant to share.

Carl frowned. "Off it how? Why?"

Willy lifted his hand and pointed uphill, off trail, into a tangle of spruce and undergrowth that looked like nothing at all. "There are foot paths up there. Old access lines. You won't see them through the snow." He paused, then added, quieter, "We're close to a road. Better going that way than staying down here."

Mara felt it then—the note under his calm. Fear. The kind that comes when someone decides the ground itself has turned dangerous.

Willy dropped his hand. "This trail isn't safe."

It landed heavy. Mara felt the space it opened— Brenna's eyes narrowing, Carl stiffening, Carly shivering harder though she said nothing. Gwen hugged her arms closer, glancing between faces as though searching for a cue. Always waiting, Mara thought. Always looking outward before she decides who to be.

Snow thickened into heavy flakes, drifting down with a muffling hush. Even voices felt muted, drawn close to the body that made them.

Carl, unwilling to let the silence sit, muttered, "Hell of a winter wonderland," his sarcasm thin and avoidant.

Brenna smirked faintly but said nothing. Carly didn't respond at all, her head tucked into Carl's side like a child.

Gwen's eyes went wide at his attempt at humor, and she whispered "jerk" under her breath, though no one seemed to hear but Mara.

Willy moved first, certain. "We're going up the rise. Phones out if you've got 'em." His tone left no space for debate.

They obeyed, gathering a blanket each from the ground before trudging up among the trees now through snow that clung in heavy cakes to their boots.

Carl muttered again—too low to be clear, but the shake of his head said enough. Carly leaned into him, her body sagging with each step. Brenna walked ahead of Mara, shoulders squared as if to prove confidence.

At the top, Willy stopped, pulling out his own phone. His phone lit—no bars, but the SOS symbol glowed. They crowded instinctively.

Carl gave a brittle laugh. "Well, this qualifies."

"Closer to the road than the camp," Willy said. "We'll walk it out, or we'll tap SOS and see what happens when you actually use that."

Mara noticed the phone as he tucked it back—a rose-gold model in a purple case, scuffed but bright. It looked almost playful in his rough hands, a human detail that didn't fit the woodsman role. Mara liked it. Proof he wasn't all flint and axes.

He scanned them, gaze quick and assessing. Carly first, pale and bound in his coat. Carl next, still flexing his injured hand. Gwen with her cut cheek and trembling arms, eyes darting. Brenna bloodied at the ear but steady, her face still turned slightly away from him, as though she hadn't forgiven him for directing them off the trail.

Mara touched her head wound again; the tacky wetness had cooled, but the ache pulsed with each heartbeat. Her knee, too, had worsened and throbbed beneath her weight.

"All right," he said. "Stay close. We're headed toward the road."

They set off, the snow falling thicker, a curtain now. Boots dragged, breaths misted, the group moving as one broken animal.

The trail was already gone. Not erased so much as folded away—hidden by the rise of land, the tight press of spruce and pine, the thickening fall of snow that blurred distance into sameness. The tractor, the trap, the wreckage where blood and diesel had soaked the ground —none of it was visible now. Just trees. Just white. As if they'd never been there at all.

The feeling unsettled her more than she expected. She kept glancing over her shoulder, half convinced the trail would reappear if she caught it at the right angle, that the world might correct itself. But it didn't. Each step carried them farther into ground that offered no reference point.

Something about it felt wrong. Not more dangerous, exactly—misaligned. As though they'd stepped out of sequence, abandoned the one known line through the woods for something improvised and brittle. She couldn't name the fear cleanly. Only that she had the sudden, persistent sense that leaving the trail would cost them later. That this was the kind of decision you only understood in hindsight, when there was no undoing it.

Another certainty pressed in alongside it: They weren't done with that place. Whatever waited back there—the wreck, the ditch, the proof that someone had meant them harm—hadn't finished with them yet. The trail wasn't just behind them. It was patient. The kind of wrong that didn't chase, only waited, confident it would be met again.

The idea settled cold in her chest: They could move

away from it for now, climb, detour, hide among trees that looked neutral and forgiving—but sooner or later, the land would bend them back. To the ditch. To the machine laid open like a carcass. To the moment everything had split.

Leaving the trail felt like a mistake.

The forest narrowed around them.

Phones glowed occasionally—Gwen fumbling hers, Brenna muttering hers was nearly dead, Carl shoving his back in his pocket with a curse. Mara had left hers in the lockbox back at her cabin—Sophie. The regret burned sharp as hunger.

When Willy finally slowed, the group closed ranks instinctively. They had entered a small clearing, ringed by trees bent under white. The air stilled here, calm and muffled, the snow falling straight.

"We'll hold here," Willy said. His voice carried low but firm.

Carl exhaled hard, tugging his scarf loose as if to show he wasn't rattled. Carly curled deeper into her blanket, eyes glazed. Gwen shifted awkwardly, trying to mirror Carly, unsure what else to do. Brenna stood apart, scanning the tree line, chin high, as though daring the woods to push closer.

Mara pulled her blanket tight. Relief flickered—then something colder. Stillness could be shelter.

Or bait. She watched Willy glance once at the dark

sky, subtle, quick—a measure of daylight, a measure of risk. No one else saw it. Mara did.

For now, the storm whispered down, muting even their pain. The world felt pocketed, enclosed. Safe or not, it felt like they had nowhere else to go.

Chapter 11

Mara hadn't meant to watch them. But the woods offered little else, and Carl and Carly always managed to fill silence whether they spoke or not.

They stood close, even in ruin. Carly's arm was wrapped in bloody bandages that looked more symbolic than medical, Carl's wrist bound with a strip of his own shirt. They had tucked themselves beneath a pine whose branches still kept some snow off the ground. The others spread wider, orbiting raggedly, but Carl and Carly clung together like twin stars fused by their own gravity.

Carl smoothed Carly's hair back from her forehead, careful not to brush the ruined arm. His voice was low—not sweet, exactly, but cultivated, as if he'd practiced tenderness until it fit him. Carly winced and smiled, wearing pain like jewelry.

At first glance it looked like devotion, reflexive as breathing. But the longer Mara watched, the more it resembled choreography—steps rehearsed until they could be done blindfolded.

"Storm's breaking," Carl murmured. "Worst of it is over, you'll see."

Willy, crouched a few feet away, didn't even raise his head. His beard was crusted white, his jacket liner stiff with frost, but his mutter came steady, as if spoken to the trees themselves: "This storm has days in it."

The words hit harder than they should have. The storm seemed to lean closer, shoving needles of snow sideways into the hollow. Each gust erased the tracks they had left behind them. Mara hated how it felt—less like weather, more like intention.

A blizzard. The word tasted like collapse.

Panic skittered up her chest: What if they never reached the road, never found camp, just drifted until their bodies gave in? Her heart stumbled into its old sprint.

Willy's tone had not been casual. Someone had named danger instead of pretending over it. Willy read the woods the way other men read clocks. She trusted that.

But even relief split into layers. First: Thank God. Then: If he can read it, maybe he can outlast it. And beneath both: If he's right, we're already caught in something we can't walk out of.

If he knew the storm had days left, why bring them here instead of pressing on to the cave? On tractor, it was half an hour more. On foot, maybe ninety minutes. Hard, but doable. And yet he'd steered them toward a road that might not exist.

Maybe he was protecting them, like he'd said. Maybe the cave was farther than he'd admit. Maybe he'd read the snow differently: slabs ready to slide, gullies primed to swallow them.

But she couldn't shake the other truth: Someone had built that trap. A trench hidden under snow, waiting like jaws. Wreckage and screaming didn't erase intention. The cave's warmth wouldn't matter if someone was waiting for them there.

Was it a prank? Drunk snowmobilers with wire and too much bravado? A trap laid months ago for thrill and left like a bear snare? Or something worse—deliberate, active, watched?

She glanced at the others. Gwen stared glassy-eyed into the trees. Brenna sat apart, silence edged and sharp. No one else seemed willing to hold the weight of being responsible for the group. Easier to let Willy bear it on his own.

Still, the other thought gnawed. Willy had seen something ahead that rattled him. His finger had pointed into the trench, but his eyes had flicked upward—toward what came next. For a heartbeat, fear. Willy knew the woods, but he wasn't fearless.

And fear could mean prudence.

Or a secret the rest of them weren't ready to hear.

Or that he had no plan at all.

His confidence worked under the skin.

Which was more dangerous, she wondered, Carl's visible bravado or Willy's quiet certainty?

Her hands wouldn't warm. She flexed them inside her cheap mittens, but the ache stayed bone-deep. It felt like the storm was working into her body the same way Willy's silence worked into her thoughts: slow, invasive, impossible to shake.

Mara pressed her thumb into the seam of her mitten until the stitch bit back. Pain as proof. Body as boundary.

Without Willy, Carl would have them wander until the cold killed them. Men like him always got followed as long as their voices stayed loud. But following Willy felt less like a choice than a tether. He drew them on with silence as much as words, and Mara wanted to trust him even when her gut whispered not to.

Her gaze drifted back to the Fenwicks. Carl's jaw twitched when he thought no one saw. Carly's smile bent frantic at the edges—the same one Mara had worn through years of panic: *See? I'm fine. Don't leave.*

They were such a unit. Maybe they shared a toothbrush. And maybe that was the problem.

Then she caught it: Carly's eyes flicking past Carl, landing on Gwen. Softer there. Tender. Gwen's gaze dropped immediately. Carl noticed nothing. Of course he didn't. Mara almost smiled.

That was the truth of it—not perfection, not performance. Just people trying to hold together because falling apart alone hurt worse.

She leaned her head against the tree, bark biting through her hood, closed her eyes, and whispered where no one could hear: "Panic's another kind of marriage. You don't want it, but it won't leave."

Her chest loosened; a scrape of laughter escaped. When she opened her eyes, Carl was smoothing Carly's hair—again—and Carly leaned in, storm pressing harder, and Mara thought: *Fine. Keep sharing your toothbrush. Let's see if you're still sharing when the woods are finished with us.*

Chapter 12

Willy hadn't said why they'd stopped at the edge of the clearing. The rise at their backs cut the worst of the wind, and the leaning oaks overhead caught the heavier flakes, branches bowed under ice.

The ground was uneven but open enough to gather. Willy paced its border, scuffing at branches, fussing over a stack of damp wood as though movement alone could disguise worry. He didn't speak.

Mara drifted back a few steps, boots crunching softer as the snow thinned beneath an oak. Needles and brittle grass poked through snow, the earth exposed like an old scar in spots. She lowered herself slowly, spine pressing into the rough trunk.

The others huddled nearer to Willy, orbiting his

steady gestures. From where she sat—half screened by branches and drifting white—she felt removed, as if she'd slipped backward through a curtain. She could see them clearly, every shift of coat and breath, yet she had the sense that from their vantage, they couldn't see her.

Snow fell in heavy flakes that clung to every edge until the trees blurred into a soft white wall. Depth vanished. What had been forest became a flat backdrop of static, a world shrinking inward. Sound dulled, swallowed, leaving only their immediate movements.

The storm was remaking the world into something small, smothering—and staring into the white long enough made her fear disappearing with it.

Carl crouched in front of Carly, carving a shallow hollow with his gloves, like order could be restored by reshaping snow. He kept glancing at her, jaw clenched, fear threaded through the mask of practiced composure. His movements had become reflexive deference—checking her, then Willy, waiting for cues.

Carly looked hollowed out, eyelids cinched, jaw locked. Willy's coat swaddled her ruined arm, but the bundle twitched with every unseen throb, each spasm rippling through her shoulders. Pain radiated from her like heat, but she made no sound. No pleas. Just rigid defiance, as if will might hold her body together where flesh failed.

Carl shifted closer, hip brushing her side. The contact jolted her. Carly's eyes flew open—wide, furious, lips peeling back in a raw snarl. Then, just as suddenly, her expression cracked into something softer, almost apologetic, recognition flickering through the haze.

Drops fell when Carly stilled—thin red punctuation on white. Mara couldn't tell if they came from the puncture in Carly's thigh or the raw strip of her arm. It didn't matter. The drops lit the snow like signal flares before new flakes smothered them. White reclaiming red. Hurt erased as soon as it appeared.

Gwen sat off to the side, head bowed, hands shielding her face. Her shoulders tremored with tiny spasms she couldn't control. When she finally peeked through her fingers, her eyes darted not toward the group but outward—into the shifting weave of trees. Wide, raw, hunted. Eyes made not from beauty but survival.

Brenna crouched closest to Willy, knees tight to her chest. Her face stayed unreadable, the mask of someone trained not to leak fear. But her eyes betrayed her. Mara followed the small cuts of Brenna's gaze—from Willy's hands to Carl's back to Gwen, then to Carly. One by one, Brenna seemed to count them, steady and deliberate. Not concern or tenderness. Presence. A soldier's check.

Willy never stilled. Clearing snow from logs. Brushing bark. Kneeling, rising, kneeling again. Always touching something. If the work was partly for fire and partly for order, Mara saw the deeper truth: Silence frightened him too.

A sound reached Mara faintly—soft, broken crying. A subdued sob. She scanned them again. Not Carly. Not Gwen. Not Brenna. Not Carl. Not Willy.

The sob came again.

It was hers.

Her hand flew to her mouth, but the tears kept sliding hot into her collar. She drew her knees closer, trying to hold herself in. Overstimulation had finally broken her open—the snow hitting her coat like static, the flare of Carly's blood on white, the storm pressing silence against her ears. Too much. Too bright. Too loud.

Her mind jumped, unbidden, to Christmas Eve a few months ago. Her parents and cousins gathered in a warm living room while she stayed in her apartment, "sick." In truth she'd done nothing—avoided everyone.

A medical billing specialist, no partner anymore, not even a bad date in ages. Parents who called but didn't know what to ask anymore. A life narrowed to work, groceries shopped for and delivered by someone else, empty weekends, and fear.

And here she was again—apart—watching others busy themselves, convinced they wouldn't notice if she slipped behind a tree.

The tears came harder, though soft. She watched

through the blur—Carl bent over Carly, frantic and helpless; Carly rigid with pain she refused to voice; Gwen hunched and trembling; Brenna counting people like inventory; Willy moving through the clearing with the burden of more than weather.

None of them whole.

Not one.

The storm had cut deeper than skin or bone—it had spread into the way they looked, breathed, moved. Into who they were now.

She tried to let the thoughts settle the way her therapist had once taught her: Storms don't answer to willpower. You don't stop them. You shelter. You prepare. Then you wait. You stay. You help each other through.

She had always liked that last part—help each other—but watching them now, she wondered who decided what help actually preserved.

Snow hissed through the oak and pine, gusts sweeping away their tracks as fast as they pressed them down. By morning, the clearing might look untouched—as if none of them had ever stood here at all. The thought snagged at Mara: If night caught them here, would they disappear entirely? Bodies softened into drifts, outlines blurred until nothing remained but white.

She wiped her sleeve across her face, surprised by the number of tears it caught.

The storm would keep coming.

And with it, she sensed, the slow erasure of trail, of direction, of self.

They'd be in these woods until the storm passed.

If they left at all.

Chapter 13

"Willy—where are you going?" Mara heard her own voice before she felt it, too sharp, too needy. He didn't pause. "Firewood."

He vanished into the trees like someone already half gone. The others pulled closer—instinct, not camaraderie. Cold had finally beaten their shared heat; breath leaked from them in uneven plumes.

Panic rose in Mara's throat—not theatrical anxiety but the old animal kind: *What if he doesn't come back?*

Snow thickened from decoration to sentence. Flakes fell in curtains, erasing edges, muting sound. The world drew inward; the clearing felt smaller every minute.

Then—branch cracks. Willy reemerged, arms full of crooked limbs: more salvaged debris than fuel. He arranged them with a quiet competence, leaving air between each piece, thumbed flame into another strange fire-starter block.

It hissed and sagged, bleeding fire until the pile caught and birthed a new orange coin in the weather.

They bent toward it—six silhouettes in a tightening ring, storm coiling harder around them.

The flame was too thin to comfort—light cut their faces instead of warming them. Mara remembered the first fire: the laughter, the scrape of spoons, the tin-can feast, the momentary illusion of fellowship in light's trick.

That illusion was gone.

Now their circle looked ruined: Carly's shallow breathing, Gwen's fearful quiet, eyes refusing to meet one another.

Sophie flickered through Mara's mind—the foolish little fire ring outside her cabin, the way she'd fed it wrong and fled inside as if the dark could lunge. That had been performance.

She shivered.

"Going for the road," Willy said, already rising.

Carl jerked upright. "Alone?"

"I move faster alone." Willy didn't soften it. "With luck, I'll find help and be back by dark. If not, I'll hit the SOS and walk back here."

His hand brushed his rose-gold phone in a purple

case. "Either way, this fire stays lit. It's your lifeline. Keep feeding it."

He knelt once more, not giving instructions so much as passing on ritual: "Dry wood first. Wet wood close till it steams. Rotate inward. Don't smother it."

His experience of countless fires gifted because he had to leave something. Carl nodded too fast. "We've got it." Then his eyes flicked to Willy's face, seeking approval.

Behind them, Gwen shifted, one arm clamped over her belly. "I... I have to pee." The words apologized for existing.

Brenna was already rising. "I'll go with you."

Carly lurched up, pale. "No. I'll take her." She pointed to the trees and brightened her voice impossibly. "C'mon, sis. Potty." The word was wrong. Infantilizing, sharp.

Gwen flinched. "Carly—"

Carly said, voice flattening, "Now."

Brenna's mouth thinned but she let them go, shadowing their first steps. Mara watched Carly's shoulders hitch with pain, the pair dissolving into white—shapes, smudges, nothing.

Mara stood, angling the opposite way—her own body's demand unmistakable. "You want me to come?" Brenna called—not tenderness, field logic. Pairs survive.

The offer hit too deeply. Mara hated the choreography of shared vulnerability, the unspoken etiquette of women in woods.

Her body locked harder. A therapist had once named it: pee shyness—flesh refusing to obey. And doing it beside Brenna felt impossibly intimate—too exposing, too imagined.

"No," she said. "I'm fine."

Brenna studied her, gave a neutral nod, turned away —but not before sweeping the clearing with that efficient sentry gaze: Carl at fire, Willy preparing to leave, Gwen and Carly vanishing for a piss, Mara departing for the same. Inventory, not affection—but something like care, disciplined and square.

Mara walked until firelight became smear and storm swallowed the sound of its crackle. Alone, the snow sounded louder than voices—constant, soft, inescapable.

She crouched, breath fogging. Relief came hot—and so did the breaking. Her throat opened. Tears came again, unsteady, steaming in the dark. She let them, shame unwinding like its own heat. Storm outside; storm inside.

When empty, she didn't return. Not right away. She moved the way lost things pretend otherwise—a slow semicircle, keeping the faint orange glow in sight without fully turning toward it.

A gust hit the oaks; snow fell thick enough that the glow pulsed, then winked out entirely. Her stomach dropped. She stepped faster, breath snagging—until the light blinked back: small, stubborn. *Fear of erasure*, Dr. Hill would say. *Of being unmade.*

When she reached the clearing, Carly and Gwen were back, standing but hunched over the fire. No one looked up at Mara. No one asked why she'd been gone so long or why her face was puffy from tears.

Carl knelt feeding the flame, eyes flicking between the fire and the trees where Willy had vanished as if toggling between altar and absent god.

Brenna stood sentinel at the perimeter, hood iced, lashes jeweled with flakes she didn't wipe away. She was making herself a post in the weather.

Heat from the fire licked Mara unevenly—hot where it touched, cold where it didn't—like a hand too large to hold her. Her shoulders let down a degree. Dr. Hill would call it co-regulation—nearby nervous systems syncing without consent.

Sparks climbed and vanished. Willy's absence thickened. Time dulled, then blurred. *Back by dark*, he'd said.

Mara watched the place Willy had disappeared until it blended with all the other blankness around them.

She didn't have a watch. But she didn't expect him

to come back anymore. None of them did, not really. Though no one would speak it yet.

Snow thickened. The fire's circle shrank. And the dark white of the storm took another slow bite out of the world.

Chapter 14

The fire had sunk low, the wood hissing instead of crackling, and the clearing seemed to fold tighter around it. The storm pressed in from every side, but the flame still held—a small point of orange in a field of white.

Mara tightened her blanket and glanced across the ring. Brenna stood at the very edge of the fire's reach, back turned, the hood of her coat slipped just enough to show a pale band of ponytail. Frost had stiffened the strands into slight arcs, like bent glass.

"Hey?" Mara said as she stepped closer. The word felt fragile in the hush, as if it might break on the air. She didn't even know what she meant by it.

Brenna's shoulders rose and dipped—a shrug more weary than dismissive. "Hey." A beat. "It's been a very long day." Her voice was steady, almost observational.

Mara bent and picked up two small branches—not sure they were worth burning, only needing something to do. Brenna mirrored her, crouching to gather damp wood that barely passed for fuel. For a moment they stood in awkward symmetry, arms full of twigs too small to matter, unsure whether to feed the fire or simply hold them.

Maybe the point wasn't the wood.

Mara let herself watch her. Closely.

Yes, Brenna was small—but the word missed the important parts. Her strength was arranged in clean, useful lines, her posture grounded even on treacherous snow. She didn't move like Carl (heavy) or Carly (dragged) or Gwen (tense). She moved like someone the woods had built: compact, quiet, fitted to the terrain.

Her boots fell silent where others stomped.

Her movements were practiced—not performative —born from repetition. She crouched without fumbling, rose without wobble. A body used to carrying weight, doing work, navigating cold seasons alone. Mara's gaze drifted upward. Brenna's face caught only half the firelight, the other half swallowed by storm-dark, giving her a carved look—one side fierce, the other missing.

Her lashes were iced, but her eyes still shone beneath, catching the flame like coins. They were too sharp to stare at directly. Every time Mara did, she felt the urge to glance away, as though looking too long would reveal something she wasn't ready to know.

Even the ponytail held its discipline, clipped tight despite snow and sweat. Mara thought of her own hair—matted with blood and ice—and hated the comparison but couldn't stop making it.

Brenna shifted the branches in her arms, and Mara noticed her hands—calloused where they should be, nails short, grip sure. The hands of someone who knew rope, knives, tools. Not delicate. Not soft.

One branch snapped crisply in Brenna's grip. Mara flinched at the sound. Brenna didn't. She just shifted her load, patient, like breaking wood in the dark was as ordinary as folding laundry.

The silence between them stretched—waiting, not empty. Mara realized she didn't want to break it.

They stepped forward at the same moment and fed their small branches into the dwindling fire. The wood hissed, steamed, curled black at the edges.

They didn't back away. They just stood there—near enough that Mara felt Brenna's presence: a shoulder's worth of heat, a stance that radiated steadiness.

Not touching.

Just near.

Brenna still didn't look at her. She kept her gaze on the fire. But their shared moment echoed in Mara's mind, heavier now. It had been recognition.

And for the first time that night, Mara's panic loosened—not because the storm had eased, not because the fire brightened, but because Brenna existed. Small, precise, competent.

For a breath, that was enough.

Mara caught herself staring and tore her eyes back to the flame, letting the quiet settle again.

The wood hissed. The circle breathed. The storm pressed on.

Chapter 15

It was fully dark now.

Hours had passed since Willy left—how many, no one wanted to guess. Too many.

The blizzard had swallowed the sky long before sunset, smothering even the idea of where light had been. It might have been eight o'clock, it might have been eleven. Mara didn't care. The only thing that mattered was that it was night. Not fading dusk, not almost night—night in full, black and suffocating, the fire the lone proof the world still existed.

They all knew it. Willy was overdue. Badly.

They had taken to shoving snow outward with one of the blankets, building a low ridge to bend the wind. It wasn't much, but it made the fire feel less vulnerable—almost like walls, almost like safety.

The wood cracked, sparks snapping upward. Brenna's voice came quiet but steady: "I don't think he made it."

No one answered. Carly stared at nothing, her ruined arm swaddled in Willy's coat. Carl twitched, jaw tightening.

"You don't see it, do you?" His voice climbed, sharp. "He walks out without a scratch. Only one of us fine." He leaned forward, eyes fierce.

Silence. Gwen's eyes narrowed in the firelight, but she stayed quiet. Mara pressed her hand against her swollen knee; every movement sent pain lancing up her thigh.

Carl pushed on. "Think about it. He knew where that ditch was. Maybe he rigged it. Maybe we're sitting here waiting while he—"

"Stop." Brenna cut him off, flat.

And then a sound split the night.

Not the crack of kindling—bigger, heavier. A branch giving underfoot. Close. Deliberate.

They froze.

The fire hissed, its light touching only the nearest trees. Everything beyond was suggestion: a sway that might be branch, a bulk that might be trunk. Mara's breath hitched. Her mind pasted shapes into every shadow—faces, outlines, figures vanishing when she blinked.

Mara held her breath. And swore she heard another

one layered over it. Breathing.

The woodpile was low. Five or six small logs left, steaming faintly. Maybe an hour if they rationed it.

"What about more wood?" Gwen whispered. "We'll need it."

The thought of leaving the circle was a blade to the ribs. The dark beyond wasn't just dark—it felt alive.

Another snap. Louder.

Carl hissed, "We're being watched."

Gwen shook her head. "It's a branch. Snow. Blizzard. Nothing else."

"You don't believe that," Carl said.

Mara's knee throbbed harder, nausea curling at the edges of her throat. Her eyes flicked to the woodpile—shrinking fast.

"We need more," Brenna said quietly. "If the fire goes out, we don't make it to morning."

Carl gave a short, joyless laugh. "So who's going? Because I'm not marching into whatever that was."

And then Mara heard herself say it: "All of us. Together."

No one laughed.

Gwen whispered, "Too loud. Too slow. If someone is out there..."

"Pairs are worse," Mara snapped. "Two go out means two don't come back."

The words hung there. No one corrected her.

Carly whimpered, shifting her arm. The sound broke the tension.

Brenna steadied them. "We stay at the edge. All of us. Pull what we can reach. No one out of sight."

It wasn't a good plan. But it was something.

They rose stiffly, hurting, moving together like a single wounded thing. Shadows stretched as they shuffled into the tree line, hands brushing shoulders, blankets scraping, the storm hissing around them.

The work was clumsy. Carl's ruined hand scraped uselessly at branches he couldn't grip. Gwen staggered with each tug, her cheek glinting red. Carly bent once, teeth clenched, dragging back a stick with her good hand. Brenna steadied her, blankets brushing like tethered wings. Mara limped painfully, but the nearness of the group pushed her forward.

Behind them, the fire dimmed—first dull, then gone, swallowed by the storm.

Mara turned and felt her chest hollow. No glow. No anchor. Just blank white.

"Light," Carl snapped. He fumbled his phone out, thumb shaking. A harsh LED beam knifed through the trees. Snowflakes flared like sparks. Relief, thin but immediate.

"My phone's almost dead," he warned. "We finish now."

They rushed—grabbing, hauling, snapping deadfall.

The flashlight bobbed, blinding more than guiding. Still, they worked faster.

Then the light died.

A gasp rippled through them. The world went utterly black, their eyes crushed to pinpoints. Snow swallowed all shapes. They groped blindly for one another—hands on shoulders, on sleeves—just to be sure they weren't alone.

Gradually, Mara's sight returned. Trees swam into focus. And then she saw it: A faint pulse of red, low to the ground.

Coals. Alive.

"There," she whispered.

They stumbled toward the dying fire, dragging branches like offerings. The coals hissed, sulked, refused to catch—until a twig flared, then another. Flames nipped, then climbed, then leapt. Within minutes the fire was alive again, crackling hot, shoving the storm back a few precious feet.

They fed it greedily. Branch after branch until the blaze roared tall. The fire painted their faces raw, shadows cavorting around them.

For a moment they stood shoulder to shoulder, breath fogging, relief crashing through them.

Carly let out a jagged little laugh. Gwen wiped her face quickly. Carl swore under his breath—almost reverent. Brenna stared into the flames, eyes fierce, reflecting it doubled.

Mara felt her chest swell—not from warmth or victory but from the strange force of togetherness pressing in. Their pile of wood stood high now, a small mountain of survival.

For the first flicker of time that night, they had won something.

Chapter 16

The fire had grown larger than Mara thought possible given the heavy snow.

They'd dragged back so much deadfall, hauling branches loose in a rough rhythm, each of them contributing even in their ruined states. The group had built a crooked pyramid over the smoldering core, and the new wood caught. She'd expected the blaze to choke under the wind; instead it swelled, rising higher.

She had almost no frame of reference. A few birthday candles, an occasional gas stove—that was her whole history with flame. Well almost.

She'd never camped, never sat with friends around a ring of stone. The size of this fire unsettled her. The flames bent sideways in the wind, roaring when the gusts hit, then snapping back taller, as if the storm itself fed them. Heat came in waves—blasts so strong she had to lean away, cheeks flushed, only to pull close again as the cold clawed tighter. Dizzying.

Uncomfortable in a strangely comforting way.

They'd managed something like a system. Carl used a heavy, arched branch, wide as a scythe, to sweep drifts away from the circle, keeping the fire from being smothered. Scoop, toss, stamp. Return to the group, sit, then rise again when the snow crept in. Each time he stepped away, they shuffled tighter, shoulder to shoulder, as if the circle might lose its shape without him.

Blankets were wedged under them and over them— one thin layer between ice-packed earth and hips, another pulled high across shoulders and ears. Their bodies did the rest, heat trapped and passed along in a chain.

Around them, the snow they'd cleared rose into a low wall. Even sitting, it only reached their waists, maybe a little higher, but the firelight made it feel monumental. Beyond it, the glow fell off into nothing. When Mara stared too long, it felt like they sat on the lip of a precipice—fire balanced on an edge, darkness yawning beyond.

Sporadically, she saw faces in that dark. Flashes, auras, tricks of light.

More than once she could have sworn she saw

Willy's face there—wise, worn, a cold warning. She blinked it away, annoyed at herself.

The wind grew louder. It didn't sing or whistle. It howled—deep-throated, dragging along the treetops until the branches seemed to groan. Every so often a gust leaned low and forced smoke sideways through their huddle, spitting sparks into the snow. They flinched each time, afraid the fire would collapse. Instead, the flames hunched, then roared back higher, licking greedily, demanding more wood.

Mara had never thought of fire as something communal. Sophie's little fire ring blaze outside the cabin had sputtered alone, hers to tend, hers to fail.

This one belonged to no one and everyone, a shared center. She wasn't sure she deserved to sit inside its circle, but the heat didn't care.

"What's brown and sticky?" Carly asked. Her voice was flat, almost too calm, eyes fixed on the flames as she poked at them with a branch.

Silence held the question a long beat. Then Brenna barked a laugh, loud and sudden in the storm-muted dark. Carl's mouth twitched, then cracked into a grin. Gwen giggled, grabbed a branch from the pile, and tossed it in.

"What's brown and sticky? A stick," she said, shaking her head.

"Dumb," someone muttered.

"Dumb," they agreed. They loved it anyway.

Carl leaned back against the snow wall. "Brown and sticky? Caramel rolls. Fresh out of the oven."

"Pancakes with maple syrup," Gwen said.

Brenna wrinkled her nose. "Peanut butter. Off the spoon."

They groaned, argued, embellished. Hunger pushed them into memory—favorite dishes, ridiculous combos, anything to outdo the last. Carl swore nothing topped ribs slathered and falling apart. Gwen would trade her boots for pierogi stuffed with potato and onion. Brenna closed her eyes as if she could already taste ramen, broth salty and thick.

Carly sat quiet a moment, then said, "I'd kill for fries. A paper basket full. Grease bleeding through the bottom."

That one landed. Even Mara felt it, her stomach cinching. She didn't add hers aloud—grilled cheese with tomato soup, bread just at the edge of burning—but she held it close.

The food talk bled into other stories. Gwen leaned closer to Carly, her hand brushing her sister's blanket. "Remember Uncle Joel? The survival challenge up north? Middle of winter, northern Minnesota."

Carly's grin was faint but real. "God, yeah. How many nights did he last? Ten?"

"Eight," Gwen said. "He claimed ten, but Aunt Meg swore he called on day eight, begging for pickup."

"Figures," Carly murmured. "She divorced him, didn't she?"

"Meg divorces everyone," Gwen said, and for a moment they both laughed—brittle but genuine.

Brenna tilted her head, listening, genuinely curious, leaning in like she wanted to understand the sisters' shorthand.

As the laughter thinned, Carly's good hand slipped free of her blanket and found Gwen's. She didn't squeeze hard—just enough that Gwen startled, then let her face soften, the fear easing for a breath. Mara caught the moment and felt it. Even bloodied and flayed, Carly reached outward. Even terrified, Gwen let herself be held.

Mara sat silent, listening, the rhythm of their voices wrapping around her with the heat. They weren't friends. They were strangers bound by fear and circumstance.

Their guide was gone. The trail had vanished. The woods were unfamiliar and tonight utterly unforgiving.

And yet.

She found herself believing that if she drifted toward sleep—absurd as that seemed—someone would watch. Someone would feed the fire. If danger crept in, they would rouse her, stand over her, claim her as part of their circle. If she fell, became more broken than she already was, they might even care for her.

Were they good? As good as humans could be expected to be, she answered: flawed, frightened, frayed at the edges.

But human.

The storm clawed at their backs, and the fire demanded more wood, but for a flicker, their voices warmed the dark.

Mara eased herself down onto her side, folding a wool blanket lengthwise beneath hip and shoulder until it felt like a thin barrier between her and the frozen ground.

The fire breathed along her face—too close, then just enough—depending on how the wind leaned the flames. She set an arm across her ribs, feeling the rise and fall of her own breath, as if she had to remind herself she was still here.

Across from her, Carl and Carly pressed back-to-back, their outlines welded by firelight into a single shape. They weren't asleep—she could tell by the flicker of their eyes when the flames snapped—but they were still, heads bowed, lids lowered.

Not sleeping.

Resting.

Watching.

Gwen had curled inward too, knees bent, face

turned toward the circle. The firelight softened the gash on her cheek, making her features look almost peaceful, almost pleasant to look at.

Brenna was closest. Mara felt the press of her thigh, crossed and resting just above where Mara's head tucked under her hood. The contact was steady, unthinking, as though Brenna had forgotten she was even there. Mara felt it like an anchor, a warmth separate from the fire, pressing through the wool.

She noticed how the circle had arranged itself—who sat where, who faced outward, who was watched without realizing it.

For the first time since the wreck, Mara felt the strange weight of being kept safe. Not by fire, not by snow walls—but by people. She floated in the circle, half outsider, half claimed, and the thought unsettled her almost as much as it comforted her. Families did this, she supposed.

This wasn't earned. It was borrowed.

But borrowed warmth still warmed.

The storm continued around them—gusts that bent the flames sideways, bursts of snow rattling the low wall —but inside the ring, bodies and heat stitched together into something improbable. Not fully safe, not really. But close enough that Mara's mind could slip.

She let her eyes close. Darkness wasn't absolute; it flickered red through her lids, breathing with the fire.

Voices had gone quiet. The fire roared. Her body loosened, bone by bone, until she felt less like she was lying in snow and more like she was drifting above it.

She felt protected.

Mara drifted closer to sleep than she meant to.

Chapter 17

It was light before Mara realized it.

Not morning light—no gold, no warmth—just a flat gray pressing against her lids.

She lay still, afraid to open her eyes and lose the illusion. For a moment, she felt nothing but weight and warmth: the wool blanket beneath her spine, the faint memory of Brenna's thigh where her head had rested.

She had slept. Dreamless. Whole. Impossible—and yet here she was.

When she opened her eyes, the storm had not left. Snow fell in sheets. The wind had found an animal howl in the trees, shuddering over their low-packed wall until the ground itself trembled. The fire was gone, coals buried under a crust of white.

Their circle had held, though—its hollow sparing

them the worst of the gale. For all their ruin, they had done well.

Morning gray was endless. Neither bright nor dim. Day hadn't arrived so much as stalled, trapping them in a single, colorless moment. The world had become a blur without edges—sky and ground smudged into the same shifting plane, gray swallowing distance whole.

Carly had moved. Gwen held her close now, rocking slightly, eyes fixed on the hollow where the fire had been. Carly's face was pale, lips cracked blue, but when her gaze met Mara's, she managed a thin, brittle smile.

Carl paced slow arcs along the edge of their circle, boots biting into the snow. His eyes swept the tree line, then the horizon, then back again—like movement itself might summon direction from the storm.

And that was when Mara saw it.

A snowy owl perched atop a drift at the far edge of the clearing. Its body vanished against the storm, but its face—flat, perfect—glowed like a lantern in the gray.

She froze.

Last night she'd thought she saw Willy's face in this spot but blamed firelight, a trick of flame. But this was real. Solid. Unblinking.

Its yellow eyes locked straight into hers.

As if it had been there all night.

Watching.

Carl stopped pacing. "He went that way," he said, pointing into the blur of trees. "Over the rise."

They stood in the gray silence longer than they meant to. Their breath rose in thin wisps. Hunger finally registered not as discomfort but ache. No one had eaten since before the wreck. Snow could be sucked for water, but it seemed to sharpen thirst.

Mara hadn't expected winter to strip her so dry. Every gust scraped something from her—moisture, heat, breath. Her lips cracked when she moved them. Her tongue clung to the roof of her mouth. Even her nostrils burned.

Carl patted his coat. "My phone's dead."

We remember, Mara thought.

Gwen fumbled in her pocket, producing four sticks of gum in a crumpled sleeve. She held it up, apologetic. Brenna took one, broke it in half, and passed the other piece to Carly without asking.

They tried the math. How far had they walked yesterday? A mile an hour? Less? Three miles? Four? And no sign of anyone—no tracks, no ruts, no smoke, no fences. Nothing.

Brenna stirred. "We should head back toward the trail. Roads lead somewhere."

"Can you even find it?" Carl asked—sharper than Mara had heard from him before.

Brenna hesitated, then half shrugged. "Maybe. Not in this."

"I'm telling you, Willy went that way," Carl insisted, jabbing toward the trees.

Mara watched him. His voice carried conviction, but his eyes flickered—no surer than Brenna's shrug.

No one moved. The storm pressed them, demanding an answer neither direction could give.

Finally Mara said, "Maybe both are right. If Willy passed through, there'd be tracks. We look for them. If they're there, we follow. If not..." She let the rest drift.

The owl hadn't moved.

Still staring.

Still waiting.

She wondered, distantly, how this would be remembered—whether anyone would mention the owl at all.

They trudged out of the circle, snow climbing to their knees in places. Every plunge tore a gasp from Mara. The heat from sleep had already fled her limbs.

Then the trees opened ahead of them—another small clearing, deeper snow, a faint dip in the land.

And they saw it.

A shape at the tree line—dark, too still, wrong.

Willy.

He stood—no, *was held*—at the edge of the woods. As if arranged there. Waiting for them to find him.

Chapter 18

Dr. Hill:

You were supposed to try the vomit video in the restaurant. What happened?

Mara:

I couldn't. I ordered water, sat there, but I kept scanning. Every table. Who looked pale, who was eating too fast. Bathrooms, trash cans, napkins—like I was plotting escape routes.

Dr. Hill:

That's your nervous system doing its job—vigilance. But it's also how fear keeps its grip.

Mara:

I know.

Dr. Hill:

Let's try something different. We
can do the homework here. If you
want, close your eyes. Picture the
restaurant. You don't have to. You
can stop at any point—your
choice. Or—you can keep going,
and we'll sit there together. What
feels right?

Mara:

...Okay. Let's try.

Dr. Hill:

Where are you?

Mara:

Back wall. Corner booth. I can
see everything.

Dr. Hill:

Good. Stay there. Details—what
do you smell, hear, see?

Mara:

Fried food grease. Plates
clattering. Voices overlapping. It's
too bright, too close.

Dr. Hill:

Hold it. And then—it shifts. A man
across the room lurches forward.
His face drains. You hear it: the
heave, sudden, wet, echoing.

Mara:

I can't—

Dr. Hill:

Stop or continue. Your choice.

Mara:

...Continue.

Dr. Hill:

He vomits, loud, sharp. Smell hits
you—acid, bile. Your throat
tightens, crawls up your chest.
And then—it happens in you.
Heat at the back of your throat.
Sour taste flooding. Muscles
convulse. You vomit. Let yourself
feel it.

Mara:

It's on me. On the floor. People
are staring. Pity. Disgust. I'm
shaking. I can't breathe. I'll die.

Dr. Hill:

Awful. Horrid. Yes. But test it. Are
you physically dead?

Mara:

No.

Dr. Hill:

Say it.

Mara:

I didn't die.

Dr. Hill:

Good. Now scan the room, if
willing. Every face.

Mara:

Some look away. Some laugh.
Someone whispers. A waiter
grabs napkins. It's—unbearable.

Dr. Hill:

Unbearable. And yet you're still
here. Breathing. Alive. Now
another choice: stay seated or
leave.

Mara:

Leave.

Dr. Hill:

Then leave. But not running.
Running is panic's posture. Walk.
Look back once more. Take in the
room, even the ones staring. Then
walk out. That's choosing, not
fleeing.

Mara:

…I look back. And I walk.

Dr. Hill:

That's the work. Not shrinking the
fear. Walking into it, then out by
choice. Panic doesn't get the last
word—you do.

Dr. Hill:

I see you shaking. Still shaking,
but less. That's allowed. Shaking
comes, shaking goes—you're the
one it happens inside of. You're
the context, Mara. Not the
symptom.

Dr. Hill:

I saw tears. You were crying when
you chose to keep going. Why?

Mara:

Because I don't want it to own me
anymore. I want… I want my life
back.

Dr. Hill:

That's it. That's values talking.
Fear screams "survive," but
values whisper "live." And today
—you chose live.

Dr. Hill:

Want to hear something ordinary
about vomiting?

Mara:

…Sure.

Dr. Hill:

Every species does it. Reflex,
protective. The body forcing out
what it thinks will harm it. Messy,
miserable, but not usually lethal.
The phobia begins when the mind
welds catastrophe onto that
reflex.

> **Mara:**
>
> It feels like I'm getting worse.
> Even here.

> **Mara:**
>
> But who fears it everywhere they
> go? I wasn't always like this. I
> used to eat around people. Now
> just watching someone chew
> makes me brace.

Dr. Hill:

That's phobia's way. It spreads.
From one seed into a field. Not
weakness—wiring. And wiring can
be retrained.

Dr. Hill:

Do you remember the knife work
we did?

> **Mara:**
>
> I'd almost forgotten. It's better,
> actually. A lot.

Dr. Hill:

At first you could barely sit with
the picture of a butter knife. Now?
Changed. Do you remember what
else you rated high then?

Mara:

Needles.

Dr. Hill:

And how afraid are you of needles
now?

Mara:

Lower. Much lower. Without even
touching them.

Dr. Hill:

Exactly. We never did needle
work. Fear networks, but so does
exposure. Every time you stayed
—knives, panic itself—your body
learned: "I can sit with this. I can
bear this. I can survive this." That
learning generalizes. That's why
needles feel smaller now—without
ever being in the room.

Dr. Hill:

Let's pause. You've gone far. Are
you steady enough to leave?

Mara:

Yeah. I think I'm okay.

Dr. Hill:

You've done so well, Mara. Better than you realize.

Mara:

Dr. Hill?

Dr. Hill:

Yes.

Mara:

Something felt different in the restaurant today. My fear did.

Dr. Hill:

Different how?

Mara:

It wasn't dying I feared. It was vanishing. Not dead. But worse than dying. Like being erased. Pulled apart, gutted—physically, socially, mentally. Like every memory of me, every trace of meaning, gone. That's what I felt.

Dr. Hill:

You're saying it felt something like annihilation.

Mara:

Yes.

Dr. Hill:

Humans are strange creatures.
Most panic is fear of death. Or
fear of exclusion—which the brain
codes the same as physical pain.
But sometimes we reach further.
We fear something past death.
Dissolution. Loss of continuity.
That nothing of us continues—not
even in memory.

> **Mara:**
>
> Do you want to hear something
> extraordinary about vomit, Dr.
> Hill?

Dr. Hill:

From you, Mara? Always.

> **Mara:**
>
> Humans are one of the only
> species that can vomit just by
> seeing it. Not poison, not illness—
> just the sight of someone else.

Dr. Hill:

Sometimes called the contagion
reflex? Social animals mirror
distress, but with us it goes
further. We evolved in tight groups
—families, tribes. If one person
vomited from spoiled food, the
safest act for everyone was to
purge too. Primitive protection.

Mara:

Survival by imitation.

Dr. Hill:

It seems to extend beyond food.
The same reflex fires in the
presence of gore—mutilation,
blood, a body cut open. The gut
revolts before the mind has time
to think. The body would rather
eject than risk contamination.
Ancient wiring, still alive in
modern rooms.

Mara:

When I gag, when I panic—it
thinks it's saving me.

Dr. Hill:

Yes. Even if all its saving you from
is the sight of someone else's
ruin.

Mara:

And that fear… annihilation, you
called it? That's what today felt
like. Pulled apart into nothing.

Dr. Hill:

And still—you walked back
through it. You lived. No one died.

Chapter 19

Willy faced them.

Eyes open. Glassy. Fixed—on Mara. She felt his stare strike her in the ribs like a thrown stone.

His head lolled against his shoulder, tilted in a way that looked perverse, a marionette slack in its strings.

A gash, wide and dark, slashed across his throat. Below it, bare skin gleamed—Willy stripped to pants and boots, chest exposed. At first it looked oddly clean, muscular lines catching pale light. Then her eyes dropped.

His abdomen was unzipped. Split in an X, gutted. Loops of intestine spilled forward, slick and red, dangling in the snow like ramen dropped into broth gone dark.

Brenna gagged hard, turned, and vomited into the snow. The sound of it made Mara's stomach twist, but her eyes were still locked on Willy's.

His face had been kind once. She saw it there still, faint and ruined, beneath what someone had done.

Willy's mouth had been cut with a blade at the corners and forced open—splayed brutally wide to make room for the bulk of his phone. The oversized screen was wedged with care into his face, cracked edges catching the light.

The corners of his mouth had been carved outward, cut deep into each cheek. What might have been the creases of laughter were ripped open instead, peeled back into a grotesque grin. Inverted, obscene—a maw that swallowed his own voice.

Snow clung where it landed, delicate against gore. Flakes caught in blood, in the wet shine of exposed flesh, refusing to melt, frosting ruin with white.

Mara's body betrayed her. Her throat heaved and she dropped to her knees, retching into the snow not far from where Brenna had already marked it.

Carl swore, a string of words breaking sharp in the air. Carly made no sound, only turned into Gwen's shoulder. Gwen shielded her, prey eyes blazing, jaw locked tight.

The clearing filled with the sound of their breath, of

snow hissing as it fell heavier, muffling everything but the sight in front of them.

They stared—five survivors in awe at the ruin of the man who had once been their guide.

And Mara felt the owl's eyes on her still.

Chapter 20

They didn't stay with Willy. They couldn't.

Carl pulled the satchel loose from his dangling leg, grimacing as if the bag itself might bite. They wouldn't open it. Not yet.

The phone wedged into Willy's mouth was a ruin—screen spiderwebbed, casing crushed. No saving it. Not worth touching.

Mara tried not to think about the satchel. About what might be inside—water, a candy bar, a scrap of jerky. Something that might change everything. The thought made her flush with shame. Willy was still swaying there, gutted, and already her mind was picking over his belongings.

Hunger clung harder than guilt.

They left him swaying in the tree, one arm tangled, one leg skewed, the other slumped beneath fresh snow.

The image burned behind Mara's eyes like an afterimage.

They backtracked—past the clearing, past the firepit now a hollow of ash. Every step tasted of retreat, but no one said the word. Their silence felt deliberate, a pact of denial.

They told themselves they could find the trail—the same narrow cut where the flatbed had gone down. Retrace it, walk it in reverse. Follow their own disaster back to safety.

At first the crunch of boots was steady. Sharp, rhythmic, each footfall cracking the crust like brittle bones. Then the snow thickened, the sound dulled: crunch to thud, thud to panting drag—boots sinking, snow sighing as if alive. Rhythm staggered into exhaustion.

Mara's breath caught. *If I fall, I'll never get up again.* Her knee shrieked with each lift, but worse was the thought the others might notice—might decide she was the one to abandon.

The forest pressed closer, branches bent by the gale into snarls. Snow slashed sideways, erasing tracks as soon as they formed. *What if we're circling? What if we've already passed this place?*

Carl's broad shoulders loomed ahead, the only anchor in the blur. *If he goes down?* She saw him blue-lipped, green eyes glazed, a cairn of flesh half buried in drifts.

A crack from the trees snapped them still. Wind rushed into the pause, needling cheeks raw. Then a slam: a snow-burdened limb sheared from its trunk and smashed the ground with the weight of a falling beam. A plume of white dusted their hoods. Mara imagined it striking bone instead of snow, burying them without even a cry.

No one spoke. They listened until silence became unbearable, then lurched on.

Her fingers were gone now—not numb really, absent from any feeling. She flexed them and felt nothing. *That's how it starts.* Hands, feet, then sleep. And sleep whispered, gentle as fire.

But it wasn't only cold. The storm pulled them dry. Mara's lips had split; her tongue rasped like sandpaper. Her nostrils burned with each breath. Even beneath wool and down her skin felt tight, moisture leeched straight through fabric. A frozen desert.

Sophie came to her—the little black cube, the lock on the door, heat blowing soft against her skin. She should never have left.

Safe there.

Alive there.

Instead—here, teeth chattering, skin burning.

Carly stumbled. Her blue cap bobbing through the snow. Gwen caught her, whispering something the storm immediately shredded. Mara heard what wasn't said: She won't make it. None of us will.

Boots moved again. No crunch. No thud. A dragging hush, ragged like breath through teeth.

They went.

Snow thickened. Silence with it. Every sound stolen before it finished. A branch cracked—snuffed in air. A breath—swallowed. The world collapsed to one rhythm: crunch, drag, pant. Even that dulled, consumed by white.

Mara wanted to ask if they were lost, but the storm felt like a throat waiting to gulp her words. She fixed on Carl's back. *If he disappears, we all do.*

Her mind tugged to Willy again: his face slit, his mouth filled. She forced another picture—the shy grin when he'd said "Paleozoic Plateau," the glint when Brenna laughed. Holding that memory felt like rebellion. Even if the storm erased other voices, she would keep his.

But exhaustion thickened. Memory dimmed. Her body shrank inward: legs stiff, breath shallow, fingers locked in her shit gloves. Blood retreated to her core.

Carly whimpered, a cracked squeak. Gwen murmured back, soft, strained, like rope pulled too tight.

Carl called a halt. Not loud—just firm. They gathered, huddled tight, their warmth a weak bubble against the gale. Snow packed hair, lashes, collars, melting then freezing again, stitching ice into their clothes.

Mara thought: *This is burial.*

Then came the numbers. How long since food? Since even a sip of water?

Carl's phone, dead.

Four sticks of gum, three now.

One dead man's pack, unopened.

Their entire inventory: gum, a storm, and hope running thin.

They pressed on.

The sound shifted again. No crunch, no drag. Not for a while. Only hush, a whisper—the noise of snow collapsing under its own weight. The storm stole time as it stole sound.

Mara's thoughts frayed. Her mother's kitchen light— yellow, steam on glass. Dr. Hill's carpet, the weave she stared into to keep from fainting.

The storm agreed. Louder, angrier, filling every space until thought muffled. Mara had prayed it might ease. Instead it pressed harder, as if aware of them— determined to grind them flat.

Hours blurred—or minutes stretched. Her world shrank to rhythm: left, right, drag, breath. If she'd been alone, she'd have sat down already. Let snow cover her. But Carl's shoulders, Brenna's braid, Gwen's arm around Carly—those shapes kept her upright.

Survival wasn't will. It was contagion.

The trees thinned without warning.

One step: trunks. The next: a clearing.

Not open—*exposed*. The storm laid bare.

It was only a hundred yards across, maybe less, but it might as well have been a mile of tundra. Wind whipped across with an authority that made her knees weaken, sculpting bowls and ridges that looked alien. A darker smear ahead—maybe tree line, maybe nothing. It hardly mattered.

Mara had "seen" blizzards before—from a car, from a window, from a couch with cocoa. She hadn't been *in* one. Not where wind carried knives and every breath tasted like erasure. This wasn't the inconvenience of weather. This was weather as a weapon.

Carl pressed forward, hunched, and they followed. Five steps in, Mara's chest seized with the realization of how visible they were—tiny dark figures crossing white, every outline etched sharp. The storm scoured them, flattening their hoods and hats, clawing through seams.

The storm was too much.

Back they went. Instinct, not choice.

Beaten, they angled toward the tree line, hugging the fringe like insects desperate for bark. Breath ragged, legs screaming, they crawled along the edge until Carl spotted a break—a narrow mouth in the trees, sloping down. The direction he swore the trail and wagon lay.

No one argued. Even Mara, half believing, half not, was grateful. The clearing had shown them what the storm truly was. The woods had been brutal, but out here was worse—devastation without shelter. She found herself longing for branches that cut her face. Better the forest's teeth than the storm's maw.

Wind tore Brenna's hood back, whipping her braid into ropes of ice. Carly sagged into Gwen's arms. Brenna moved stiff, purple blooming across her throat, a bruise like spilled ink.

Carl called another stop. They huddled again. No words. Their voices had been stripped away—same as tracks, same as warmth.

Mara realized she hadn't spoken in hours. Maybe none of them had. Their voices, like everything else, were forgotten in the snow.

Chapter 21

Every time a clearing opened, Mara felt it growing worse. That ancient, skin-deep knowing. Observed.

The prickle at her nape. The hairs rising on her arms despite the cold. A tightening between her ribs, as if her body were shrinking itself, trying to make less of a target.

Eyes on them. Not imagined, not hallucinated—remembered. The way animals remembered the predator before they saw it.

Her wounds pulsed with it. Each throb felt like an eye of its own, wide and raw, staring back at whatever stared at them.

She didn't look behind her. Couldn't. Something older than choice warned her: *Don't show you know you're being watched.*

Was it the woods?

The owl?

Or was it closer?

Brenna limped slightly, bruise blooming dark across her throat. Gwen kept Carly under one arm. Carl plowed ahead, shoulders squared like a shield. They were too close. Too steady. Mara wanted distance, but closeness was safety—wasn't it? Or the opposite: Maybe danger walked inside their circle.

Panic wasn't hers alone. It spread—one breath sharpening another, one suspicion feeding the next.

Fear in the Driftless wasn't personal.

It was viral.

Snow fattened in the air, heavy as soaked feathers. They didn't find the trail. Not yet. They wound up and down cuts and ridges Mara couldn't name. Coulee, gully, ravine—words blurred, terrain repeated. Every slope the last. Every tree the same.

She lost time, measuring only in steps. Her boots punched through snow that remade itself instantly, filling in behind them as though they'd never passed. Saplings leaned under weight, boughs arched like rib bones.

Once she glimpsed the carcass of a fence line, posts barely rising above the drifts. Then, the frozen hindquarters of a hare protruding from a bank—its ears stiff and blackened. Everything in the woods looked staged, placed as warnings.

Her body wanted to collapse into the throb of her wounds, but her mind reached somewhere strangely calm. Dr. Hill's quiet voice came to her: *Panic swears it will last forever, but nothing does. Even pain gives out. It burns, it rages, but it breaks eventually. Nothing holds constant.*

The snow wasn't crust or powder now—it was loose, collapsing under every footfall. Shin-deep, knee-deep. Up, sink, drag. Up, sink, drag. Their trail looked less like footprints than a wound in the white.

When Carl called a halt, none of them dared to sit. To rest here meant carving themselves into the drifts only to be swallowed again. They leaned instead—against trunks, against each other—knees trembling, snow devouring them mid-leg anyway.

Rest was illusion.

Mara pressed against a pine whose bark shed ice in scabs. Meltwater trickled inside her collar, cold burning like acid. Carly slumped against Gwen, face waxen. Brenna pressed fingers to her bruise.

Silence gathered around them. Predatory.

Carl broke it. His voice came stiff, low. "We should see what's in the pack."

He unbuckled Willy's satchel. The creak of straps sounded wounded. He hesitated, then murmured—awkward, real—"Sorry. And... thank you."

Out came a can stamped VEG, lettering faded. Gwen laughed once, humorless.

Next—a knife. Long, heavy. Not a woodsman's tool. A combat blade. The sheath peeled back to a metal so clean it seemed to drink light. Mara's stomach tightened.

Too much for hunting.

Too sharp for comfort.

Carl laid it carefully in the snow.

Then a fire-starter block, soap-like with a string wick. They all knew how quick it burned, how little margin of error it left. A waterproof matchbook—once ten, now three. Carl counted them twice. A metal lighter, forestry service emblem stamped on its wide sides. Carl thumbed the wheel. Sparks leapt, no flame. It felt like more than a tool. A relic. A charm. A memory.

At the bottom: a Field Notes journal, pages curled, ink bled. Carl opened it once, then closed it with a squeamish sigh, as though rifling through a dead man's mind were trespassing.

Mara reached for it, opened it quietly. Soil tallies. Rainfall marks. Sketches of ridges. But deeper in, the tone twisted.

One line—ink smeared but clear: *If I don't come back, will the trees remember me?* She closed it sharply, guilt pricking even as curiosity flickered. The journal felt alive. She slipped it into her coat before anyone could see.

A memory of Dr. Hill surfaced—his patients confessing violent flashes, thoughts that terrified them. He always said: *You're not alone. Everyone carries the dark in some way. The trick is not letting it drive.*

But here, with no police, no phones, no therapists—helpers and predators blurred.

Who could she trust?

They pressed on.

The storm thickened, flakes like gauze, draping the world in veils. Trunks rose like black ribs in a white lung. Their path vanished behind them, erased as they walked, as if the woods resisted every intrusion and corrected itself.

Mara felt it still—the prickling eyes.

The stalker in the storm.

Nerves humming like live wires. She knew the others felt it too—Gwen's flinch, Brenna's darting gaze, Carl's clenched jaw.

None of them said the word.

Chapter 22

The woods thinned for a stretch, the trail opening into a hollow where the wind moved more freely. Snow swirled low across the crust, veils torn apart and flung against the tree line. Their pace had slowed to a shuffle, each step deliberate.

Carly walked on her own, barely—head lowered, bad arm clutched to her body, boots dragging in an uneven rhythm. Gwen hovered close, murmuring reassurance that had no words left in it, only sound.

Carl stalked ahead, shoulders hunched, jaw tight. Mara trailed near the middle, her knee throbbing with every step. Brenna brought up the rear, eyes raking the trees as if expecting something to be following them.

The storm felt different here—less like weather, more like weight. The air pressed on their ears, muffling sound until each step seemed padded, unreal. Gusts carved tunnels through the snowpack that closed just as quickly, the woods breathing in and out. Trees groaned, ice-heavy, releasing sharp cracks that carried too far in the hush.

Mara smelled it first. Acrid, sour, sharp enough to sting even in the cold.

Not rot, not quite.

Something older, muskier.

She lifted her head, sniffed again. The musk clung to the back of her throat, and beneath it threaded something heavier, unmistakable: the sweet, sick tang of death.

At first she saw only a black dot against the drift, small and unsteady in the storm's blur. Snow swept around it, an eye in a flurry of white.

Her steps slowed.

The dot resolved as she neared.

Black fur rimed stiff, a stripe dulled to gray beneath frost. A skunk. It lay twisted on its side, half buried, one paw jutting stiff from the drift.

The belly had been torn wide, splintered ribs showing in pale arcs, edges crusted with frozen blood. Snow clung to the wound, softening the outline, but the recent violence was plain in ragged fur and splintered bone.

The stink rose sharper as the wind shifted—musk

mixed with the iron edge of old blood. Mara's stomach lurched. She stopped in the trail.

"There," she whispered.

Carl turned back, irritation raw, but his eyes followed hers. Gwen faltered too, clutching Carly's elbow as if to steady them both.

Brenna stepped forward, crouched. She brushed snow from the torn belly; her glove came away dark. The stink rolled thicker. She frowned. "That's not right. Skunks should be in dens this time of year. And nothing touches a skunk."

The wind shoved through the hollow, scouring their faces. Carly whimpered. Gwen pulled her forward. "Don't look. Just walk."

"Coyotes," Carl muttered, clipped and defensive. "Starving ones." He nudged snow over the body with his boot, not carelessly. Superstitiously. His face tightened and he murmured low—half to Willy's ghost, half to the skunk's—"Sorry." Then he moved on.

Brenna shook her head. "Coyotes don't eat this. Not unless they've got no choice." She let the snow fall over the animal, covering it like a secret.

They lingered a beat, the stink rolling over them like a verdict.

Gwen's face hardened; she scowled suddenly at Carly, muttered something the wind shredded, then strode past her sister with her chin high. Carly's expression crumpled, but Mara saw the truth under it: Gwen had carried her mile after mile and was still carrying her, even in anger. Strength dressed in scorn, but strength all the same.

They moved on, slower now, glances flicking back. Even Gwen, charging ahead, kept cutting looks over her shoulder as though afraid the carcass might stir. Carly blinked at it too, eyes clouded but not empty, as if she understood something was wrong, more wrong than she could name.

Mara kept her gaze forward, but the skunk stayed with her. Alive, a skunk was warning enough—bright stripe against black, a creature the world avoided. To see one gutted meant something had crossed that line. Something hungry enough, or careless enough, to take what should have been left alone.

She'd read once that skunks carried a kind of human meaning—respect born from avoidance. Tricksters in some stories, omens in others, their stripe a banner warning the world to keep its distance.

Her thoughts slid unbidden: Willy's body strung up, cruelty laid out in careful cuts. Carly's ruined arm, infection climbing like vines. Now this skunk, belly open in the snow.

Three messages, so far, written in flesh.

Back home in Michigan, she'd thought of Wisconsin

as tame. Bears, rarely. Rattlesnakes, almost never. Deer everywhere, harmless as shadows. Coyotes more nuisance than threat. Poisonous things were background noise; starvation was theoretical, something that took weeks. Out here, in this storm, she saw how wrong she'd been.

Wilderness didn't need predators to kill you.

It only needed indifference.

The musk thinned behind them, swallowed by wind, but the message clung longer than the smell.

Even the untouchable was no longer spared.

The wind needled harder. Mara bent into it, one arm crooked over her face. Her knee screamed with every step, but her mind wandered somewhere colder still.

She thought of something she'd researched years ago —the Yamabushi in Japan, monks who walked willingly into storms like this. Thin-robed, fasting, climbing mountains until their bodies failed.

Shugendō.

Exposure as devotion.

She'd never understood it but always wanted to. To take the cold on purpose, to starve yourself, to vanish into the white and call it holy. It had always sounded less like religion than a dare to the earth.

And yet here she was—half limping beside Brenna, Carl bent under Carly's weight, Gwen whispering into her sister's hair. A band trudging their line in the snow. Not monks, but not entirely unlike them either.

The difference was choice. The Yamabushi went to test themselves. They chose the suffering. This group hadn't. They'd been caught.

Maybe that was the revelation. The Yamabushi weren't chasing peace so much as stripping away—the reminder that nothing lasted. Not comfort. Not pain. To endure indifference was to brush against something holy. And if you vanished out there, if the storm swallowed you, you became part of that indifference.

That was the point: to face a world so cold it didn't care if you lived or died—and to come back changed.

Chapter 23

Since Willy, Mara had started counting them without meaning to. She didn't know why. She just knew their number wouldn't hold.

The path vanished again.

At first there had been a faint line through the drifts —Carl breaking it with sheer weight and will—but here the trees thickened into a snarl of pine and oak, branches bent low under ice. Snow ridged high, less drifts than barricades.

Mara kept glancing down, hoping for a track. Nothing. Just Carl's broad back and the illusion of direction.

Her legs ached with every lift. Cold seeped through her pants, burning her thighs. When Carl finally raised a gloved hand, she almost sagged in relief. He angled them toward a small thicket of pines, their needles heavy with clumped snow. Beneath the branches, the ground was nearly bare—a pocket carved by wind.

No one spoke, but everyone folded inward. Mara's knees buckled first; she sank without meaning to. The pine duff pressed soft beneath her coat, stealing her weight, tugging her toward sleep. Her eyes slipped half shut.

A shift beside her. Brenna sat too, small frame folding inward, chin to her chest. Not fragile—just spent.

Mara's lids drifted shut. She thought of Sophie—her cabin, the soft hum of heat, the locked door. A bed she didn't have to earn. She felt herself drifting toward it—

A scrape snapped her awake.

She didn't know how long she'd been down. Seconds? Minutes? The thicket was dim, the storm's light muffled by green. Brenna had changed position—knees drawn up, head raised. Mara hadn't heard her move.

Wrong.

Wrong in a way that crawled across her skin.

Then she saw Carl and Gwen a few feet ahead—both rigid, staring into the same narrow gap between trunks.

Not at each other.

Outward. Unmoving.

Mara held still. The hush was too sharp, too total. Every tiny sound magnified—the tick of snow slipping from a branch, the rasp of her coat, the hammer of her pulse.

Something moved out there. Or had moved. Snow crunched—faint, irregular. Not purposeful enough for a person. Not steady enough for an animal.

A stagger. A start. A stop.

Carl crouched lower, jaw clamped. Gwen shrank into herself, shoulders hunched. Brenna's eyes went sharp, feral. *They all heard it*, Mara thought. *They all sense it. And I don't.*

Her fingers curled in the duff. Nails scraped dirt.

She didn't breathe.

Time bent. The forest held its breath with them. A pop overhead—just a branch shedding ice—felt like a gunshot. Every gust sounded like approach.

Finally Carl whispered, so quietly she thought she imagined it: "We should move."

The words cracked the air. Gwen nodded. Brenna didn't look away. Mara swallowed—loud in her own skull—and rose slowly, carefully quiet.

They slipped out of the thicket in silence. No one said what they thought they'd heard. No one even had language for it.

It wasn't sound that had frightened them. Not exactly. It was alignment—each of them sensing the same wrongness from a different angle.

Something had noticed them.

They returned to the path—if it was a path—each step placed with surgical care. Their shapes bent low, shadows strung together by fear.

Days felt like they'd passed since Willy, though it had been only that morning. His body gutted and hung like a warning. None of them had spoken of it. Now every step felt indebted to that image.

They didn't walk softly because Carl told them to. They walked softly because anything louder felt like invitation.

Maybe someone passed while we hid. A hiker. A hunter. Someone who could have helped.

But with murder still steaming in memory, none of them believed help was coming. Whatever moved out there wasn't coming to save them.

They walked single file, slower, quieter. The hush grew thick. Mara's mind gnawed at the strangeness of it —humans hunted. Campfire story stuff. Slasher movies. Streaming thrillers.

But here, trudging through the dark woods, the absurdity fell away. Safety was new. A modern luxury. For most of human history, this—walking quiet through the dark, watched by something stronger—was the normal state.

A prickle ran along Mara's spine. Their little group— Willy, Brenna, Carly, Gwen, Carl, herself—had become a tribe. Roles unspoken but there: Carl breaking trail, Gwen guarding Carly, Brenna always scanning, Mara pulled into the circle whether she asked for it or not.

Humans were built for this. For fear. For leaning into each other when the dark pressed close.

And now they were hunted.

The storm shifted. Instead of steady veils, surges punched through the hollow, wind hitting so hard the snow stung like gravel. Mara bent forward, eyes squeezed shut. Breath clawed her throat.

They crouched without agreeing to, bodies folded into the gale. Branches exploded above them—like cracks of lightning in the canopy. Snow tore from the ground and mixed with what fell, until the air itself was white noise.

Then, abruptly, a lull.

Thin.

Temporary.

Carl's silhouette reformed. Brenna's braid. Gwen bent under Carly's weight. Just enough to breathe.

They started again.

Mara fell into the rhythm: crunch, drag, breath, pain. With unexpected moments of relief—safe in the tribe, safe in the circle.

She looked up again.

And froze. Carly wasn't there.

Not in front of her. Not behind Carl. Not anywhere. Just gone.

"Carly," she whispered. Too soft. Carl stiffened but didn't turn.

She said it louder. "*Carly.*"

Carl turned then. His face went pale—drawn, eyes wide and empty. The line halted. Gwen's head whipped side to side, frantic.

There was no Carly.

The four remaining survivors froze. The forest leaned in. The silence fell heavier than anything the storm had thrown at them.

"If you do not walk until your feet bleed, you will not see
the Buddha."
En no Gyōja

Chapter 24

They stood frozen in the trail, snow whispering through the branches, until Carl finally declared that they had to backtrack. His voice sounded scraped raw, but it was the only sound any of them made. They turned without discussion.

Their boots chewed up the path they'd just walked, prints overlaying prints until nothing could be read. The trail became churned, shapeless, a scrawl in the snow. Still they bent to examine it—Carl with his jaw clenched tight, Gwen crouching until her mittens brushed the ground, Brenna narrowing her eyes.

They searched for some sign—one print veering away, a broken branch, a sag in the snow. The path gave them nothing. Just a single rope of prints, their line, single file.

Mara crouched too, knowing it was useless. "If she left," she whispered, "she must've stepped sideways. Off into the trees."

Carl didn't answer. His gaze moved past the ground and into the spaces between trunks, as if he was less interested in tracks than in whatever might be watching.

They trudged over their own trail again. Their legs sank deeper each pass; the ground softened beneath their weight until it sucked at their boots. Snow fell heavier, filling the hollows as fast as they made them. If Carly had left a mark, it seemed gone now—flattened, as though the storm had bent down to erase her.

They went a mile. Single file, heads bent. No Carly. No print clearly hers. The futility gnawed at Mara, but she said nothing. Nobody spoke.

Silence was worse than shouting would have been. Every step was an accusation: We've lost her. But to raise their voices, to scream her name, felt wrong. Willy's body still burned in their memories, gutted and hung like a warning.

To call out was to invite it.

To admit you were prey.

So they walked hunched, eyes snapping to every tree and broken shape in the snow. Mara could feel the paranoia moving between them like fever. Carl's tension rolled in his shoulders; a breath later she felt it in her own chest. Behind her, Gwen's breaths were too shallow, too fast, as though even exhaling might draw the wrong attention. Brenna's steps stayed unnervingly light, each placement precise, and Mara found herself copying that cadence, boot after careful boot.

Careful quiet became law. It wrapped tighter than snow or hunger, binding each throat shut. To break it felt like it would crack whatever fragile crust still held them together. And yet the same quiet betrayed Carly—if she still breathed somewhere out there, she would never hear them. They could pass within twenty feet and move by like ghosts.

More than once, Mara felt a scream rise—Carly's name raw on her tongue—but she swallowed it.

When Carl finally turned back, it was without ceremony. He halted, eyes pinched, pivoted. His lips parted, as if to shout—but he shut them again and started forward, reverting to their original heading.

They again walked over their own churned tracks.

When the low pine thicket came into view—the place they'd sheltered before—her stomach folded in on itself. Twice now they'd circled it. Twice now Carly had not returned.

Time warped: another hour gone, or only minutes stretched thin by fear. The storm pressed, closing the world down. There was no horizon, just white falling into white.

Mara's legs throbbed, her knee a live coal. *I could drop here*, she thought. *Just drop and let the snow cover me.*

She forced her gaze up from the churned path and studied the others. In the half-light they all carried the same rawness, but each wore it differently. Carl's jaw was all tension, tendons sharp under skin, as if will alone might drag Carly back into view. Gwen's eyes snapped everywhere at once, wild and shiny, her body pitched forward like she might fling herself into the trees if that was what it took. Even Brenna—who met everything with that narrowed, measuring stare—looked stripped of armor. For a moment. Her gaze cut in deliberate sweeps opposite the others', scanning hollows they missed, corners they ignored, as if some instinct had assigned her the group's blind spots.

They weren't random in their frantic looking, Mara realized. Fear had organized their effort.

Carl watched the ground, hunting tracks. Gwen scanned low branches, the sag of snow where someone might have brushed past. Brenna searched the deeper dark—the gaps between trunks where absence could be alive. Each one looked where the others didn't. A system, born of panic. Without words.

And under that system, something more. They weren't only searching because Carly was Carl's wife or because Gwen had walked beside her. They searched because the group itself was smaller without her, misshapen, a body missing a limb.

She was proof they could keep one another alive.

Without her, the circle broke.

For a moment, Mara felt that tether run through her too—tight and undeniable. She had feared them, resented them, even Brenna's scrutiny. But now she understood: if one of them vanished, it wasn't only grief. It was collapse.

It was Brenna who saw it.

She stopped so abruptly Gwen nearly walked into her. Brenna crouched, brushed snow aside, then tipped her head toward the ground.

"What is it?" Mara whispered.

Brenna didn't answer, just shifted so Mara could see.

At first it was only churn: pocked white, uneven. Then Mara spotted it—a faint set of prints veering off, angling away from the main line. Not far. A small fork, a few steps only, before they curled back and rejoined the trail.

Carl bent low. "Could be hers."

"Or ours," Gwen breathed. "It's so chewed up."

Even as she said it, all four of them leaned toward the fork. Faint, imperfect, but there. A step away. A possibility.

They followed it.

They'd all felt it already: that hush in the trees, the

certainty of being shadowed. Willy's body endured in their minds, gutted and strung up like meat.

If Carly had been taken—peeled from them the way a wolf cuts a weak one from the pack—then these tracks might be less a road back to her than a lure. A thread leading straight to whatever had done the peeling.

The paradox hardened around them. Instinct screamed to scatter, to crash through the trees, to dig until Carly was back in their arms. The same fear that bound them also muzzled them.

So they moved carefully, almost reverently. Eyes down or up, voices sealed, more like people following a ritual than a trail.

The prints were shallow, easily lost in shifting powder, but they kept their heads bowed, bent like penitents, until the marks vanished again. For a moment it seemed the storm had wiped them completely.

Then they saw the glove.

Half buried, stiff with frost. Gwen snatched it up with a small gasp. "Carly's. She was wearing these."

They went on, slower still, scanning every dip and hollow. A few yards farther: her blue wool hat, crusted with snow, lying as though dropped mid-step. Another twenty yards: her coat, half buried and rigid.

Just beyond the coat, something darker stained the snow. At first Mara took it for shadow, a trick of gray on white. Then she saw the color—rust-red, frozen into the crust, flecks and smears sharp as glass.

Not a pool of blood.

Not nothing.

Drops.

The red leakage—presumably Gwen—led to a ragged mess in the drift: bandages, or what had been. Strips of cloth stiff with ice, torn and twisted as if ripped off in a frenzy. One piece was soaked through and brittle, edges curling like old scabs.

Another was still tacky where it clung to the snow. Mara pictured Carly's ruined arm, the way she held it tight to her body, and saw her clawing at the wrappings, shredding what held her together. As if the binding itself were the enemy.

Brenna crouched beside the blood, voice low, almost clinical. "She hasn't lost much. Not yet." She brushed snow aside as if checking a pulse, then stood, jaw tight.

The trail stretched on, objects scattered like breadcrumbs, each one tightening the band around Mara's chest. These weren't things you dropped by accident.

They had been shed—deliberately.

She'd heard of it, dimly—stories of people freezing who tore off their clothes at the end, convinced they were burning even as they froze. Paradoxical undressing. The brain misfiring at the end.

Now it wasn't a story. It was glove, hat, coat. Carly

peeling away into the snow. Mara imagined frost feathering out from Carly's skin, each breath turning her more statue than woman.

They walked on slower than ever.

Afraid not only of what hunted them—but of what the cold itself could teach them.

Chapter 25

In this place, the land makes no distinction. Hoofprint, pawprint, footprint—all are temporary.

The Driftless never wore the glacier's weight.

While the ice scoured every horizon around it flat, mile-thick sheets grinding down rock and memory, this pocket of hills remained.

A spared island. A wound the cold could not close.

When blood spills here, when tracks stamp briefly into snow, when a band searches in urgent stillness, the land does not flinch. The lost lose scent in a blur of rolling bluffs. The searching lose signs around corners. Traces vanish, dusted away without malice, without notice.

It is neither fast nor slow, neither violent nor gentle. This is no Arctic, not a stage of grandeur—ancient indifference. Unconcerned by what moves across its sandstone surfaces.

Sandstone outcroppings crumble at a touch—rock that appears solid collapsing under weight. Caverns promise shelter but fracture under pressure, ceilings flaking into dust.

Yet in cracks and hollows lie crystals, veined surprises that gleam like remembered fire. The land tempts exploration even as it warns against it.

Winter makes the topography honest.

The trees endure as they can. Oak and maple stand stripped and skeletal, crowns black against the sky, bark cracked as though scorched. Pine keeps its needles but not its warmth—green stiff with ice, branches bent in permanent supplication. Hemlock suffers worse, catching more snow than it can bear, bowing until boughs touch ground.

What lives is shaped by weight.

What breaks lies buried.

Life moves with caution here. Deer pick their way along ridges where wind scours snow to crust. Coyotes lope silently, ribs pressing thin, coats rimed with frost. The black bear, scarce queen of summer ravines, dwindles to rumor in these months—its presence guessed only by the hollow where it sinks itself, the silence where something still breathes.

Even these creatures seem older than themselves, as

though their blood remembers what their minds cannot. Lineages pressed thin across winters. Instinct sharpened by something deeper than hunger—by fear itself.

Storms here carry memory.

The danger is not extremity but deceit. Warmth lingers just long enough to disarm, then turns sharp—needling flesh, stiffening lungs, laying ice over every surface. Cold here is never constant—it withdraws, ambushes, returns. Its only rhythm is indifference.

Spring does not relieve so much as confuse.

The air smells of thawed soil and opened carcass—the slow leak of decay feeding back into growth.

Bluff after bluff, coulee after coulee, each one a scar left by absence. A topography rough enough to hide in.

Beneath the bluffs, water seeps through limestone and dolomite, carving chambers. Caves. These spaces are not made in years but in increments of water. Dripping, dissolving, collapsing. The stone opens slowly, a patient subtraction.

In some chambers the walls are coated with a pale crust, neither powder nor stone, a substance that clings and smears.

In winter, when the surface hardens and all motion slows, these places persist.

Above, the weight gathers as cloud. Gray heaped upon gray, dim light straining through. Snow falls without urgency at first.

Below, any trappings or marks left are ground away. Not fast. Not slow. Just thorough.

The storm lowers in layers, each stratum of cloud and drift pressing on the ridges below.

And beneath, the living stagger on. A herd cut thin across the slope, ribs showing. A band bent low against wind, their outlines nearly erased. All of them crossing a surface that does not acknowledge passage, their trails as temporary as breath.

The Driftless does not care.

Chapter 26

They found her at the edge of a clearing, crouched low, as though she'd tried to burrow into the snow for warmth.

At first Mara thought it was only rags—a bundle half buried—but then the shape jerked, a shoulder twitching. The breath ripped sharp through her teeth.

"Carly."

Carl's voice snapped the silence, rough and cracked but so forceful it made Mara flinch. He was already moving before anyone else had taken a step, boots pounding through snow and brush as though sound no longer mattered.

Carly sat bare-armed in the clearing, shirt torn down the side, sleeves shredded to ribbons. Her hair clung in frozen ropes to her temples. Heat bled visibly from her skin, thin threads of steam torn away by the storm. Her body shuddered—muscles firing in violent, uncoordinated jolts, each one trying to escape.

Her ruined arm was exposed now. No wrapping. No cover. The flesh was grotesque: angry red, black in places, skin split where swelling had burst it open. Dark streaks climbed upward like corrupted veins, blood frozen where it had run. She had clawed herself raw. Her nails were bloody, strips of skin torn from her own wrist.

The snow bore the evidence—rust-stained patches, frozen clumps, the remnants of a frantic shedding.

Carl dropped to his knees beside her, snow spraying. His gloves went to her face immediately, cupping her cheeks, forcing her to look at him. "Carly, it's me. I've got you." His voice cracked, every word dragged out of his chest.

Her head lolled. Her eyes were glassy, pupils wide. For a flicker she focused. Her lips parted. "Carl..." The sound was barely a breath, but it broke them all.

Mara crouched nearby, stomach clenched against the sweet, rotting stench rising from Carly's arm. Gwen covered her mouth with her mittens, tears freezing on her cheeks. Brenna stood back, face unreadable, eyes darting from Carly to the tree line as though already choosing what danger to watch first.

Carl pressed his forehead to Carly's. "You're not leaving me. You hear? You're not leaving me." His hands shook as he stripped off his parka, draping it around her shoulders, then tugging at his scarf, his gloves—anything that could cover her. "She's freezing," he snapped, voice edged like steel. "Don't just stand there. Help me."

Gwen dropped beside him, peeling off her own coat. Mara hesitated at the smell—but Carl's look cut through her. She stripped her mittens and shoved them onto Carly's bare hands the best she could. The skin was waxy and terrifyingly light.

Carly whimpered. "Don't... leave..."

Carl's whole frame convulsed. "Never. Never."

The forest seemed to lean in. Snow hissed through branches. Wind swallowed the sounds of their voices almost as quickly as they made them. Light thinned— late-day gray where every shadow stretched long.

The blizzard had not eased once since morning. It felt eternal, a storm with no memory of calm. And in that small, desperate circle—Carl, Carly, the others crouched around one another—everything felt unbearably human against a land that didn't care if it erased them.

Carly coughed, wet and low, flecks of dark blood bubbling at her lips. Gwen sobbed. Mara bit her lip until copper filled her mouth. The blood looked wrong—too thick, too dark, already turning.

Carl ignored it. He kissed Carly's forehead, her temple, the frozen corner of her lips. His whispers were a stream of devotion and denial. "You stay with me. Just a little longer. I'll get you warm. I'll get you home."

Mara's chest seized. He believed it—or he needed to. The force of his love bent them all toward it, a gravity she felt in her bones. Whatever decisions remained were no longer collective. They would rise and fall with Carl and Carly now. Whether it killed them or not.

Brenna broke the spell. "We can't stay here."

Carl's head snapped up, glare deadly. "Then we move. With her."

Brenna didn't argue, but the tension in her jaw spoke plainly.

Mara looked around, expecting nods. Gwen didn't even look up—already fussing with Carly's hair, tucking the parka tighter. But Brenna had gone still. Concern, not disagreement. The same cold knot that had just risen in Mara's own chest.

It wasn't that Carl wanted to save his wife. That was human. Noble. It was the way he'd said it—as though the rest of them were limbs and muscle meant only to carry her forward, no matter what it cost. As though survival itself had narrowed to one life. Hers.

Carl shifted, hooking his arms under Carly's shoulders, bracing to lift. "On three," he growled. No one had asked. "We lift."

Mara scrambled closer, hands sliding awkwardly under Carly's legs. Gwen helped too. Together they heaved. Carly cried out, a broken, animal sound that stabbed straight through Mara's ribs.

Carl hushed her, pressing his cheek to hers. "I know. I've got you."

The weight of Carly shocked Mara—too light, too heavy, brittle and sinking all at once. Her breath stuttered against Mara's arm.

"Up," Carl commanded.

He staggered to his feet with her in his arms, face contorted with strain, blood from her wound already soaking into his coat. He didn't notice. Wouldn't have cared if he did. His entire body radiated one truth: He would carry her through hell if he had to.

Mara stumbled after him. Gwen clung to her sleeve. Brenna brought up the rear, eyes sharp, scanning.

The snow closed around them, smothering sound, erasing their tracks almost as soon as they made them. Mara looked back and saw the bloody wrappings Carly had torn free—still there, but blurred, sinking into white as though the storm was grinding them under.

The trees bent and groaned like the timbers of a ship going down. Limbs snapped overhead with rifle cracks. Powder lifted in sheets that erased faces even a few feet away.

Just standing in it stung—cold that burned, cold that stripped warmth grain by grain. A patience more lethal than fury.

They had no path. No direction. Just a man carrying his dying wife into the white.

The storm pressed tighter. Daylight thinned.

Carly's breaths rattled.

Hours to live, Mara thought. If that.

Still, Carl walked. And the rest followed.

Chapter 27

The storm hit sharper than before, gusts slicing across the hollow until every breath burned. Snow came two ways at once—vertical and heavy, soft as flour, while another current blew horizontal, razors that cut any exposed skin.

Their order had become habit: Carl in the lead with Carly clinging to him, Gwen usually at her side, steadying, dragging. Mara behind them. Brenna in the rear, head on a swivel, eyes sharp, a sentinel scanning their flanks.

But Carly had become a two-person job. Her legs buckled more often, her breath dissolving into thin coughs that turned to heaves. Carl cinched her left arm tight against his ribs. Brenna took the right from Gwen, jaw set as she shouldered the weight. Freed from hauling, Gwen drifted back a little, nearer Mara.

A blast of wind screamed through the hollow, flinging snow sideways like gravel.

"Break," Carl barked. "Here. Just—here."

His words snapped off in the gale, but he dragged Carly toward the crooked V of two fallen trunks. Brenna muscled herself in beside him, both of them bending low to shield her from stinging snow spray.

Mara trailed after, chest burning, vision smeared with ice. Twenty yards off, she spotted a pine, branches sweeping to the ground—heavy with snow but knitted tight enough to make a dark pocket. She veered for it, bent double, and shoved under. The storm dulled instantly, muffled to a steady roar as if she'd ducked beneath water.

A shape turned in the blur—Gwen, hood half torn, face tight with strain. She looked ready to follow Carl, but Mara lifted a hand and motioned her over. Gwen hesitated only a moment before shoving through the drift and crouching under the pine beside her. They huddled shoulder to shoulder under the low boughs.

The difference was startling. Outside, the wind shrieked. In here, the air was still, snow hissing softly against needles.

"Better," Gwen murmured, tugging her hood forward. She touched her scalp and winced. The flap of skin there had frozen stiff, dried blood and hair crusted into a black-red shard.

Mara squinted at it. "Christ, Gwen—your scalp flap is frosted." The words came out clumsy, too loud in the hush.

Gwen's eyes widened. Then she barked a laugh—quick and sharp. Mara snorted too, a thin, involuntary sound. Humor felt indecent, with Carly failing only yards away, but it rose anyway, brittle and bright.

"Growing my own ice crystal," Gwen said, grinning crookedly. "Split ends—the deluxe package."

They stifled laughter into their sleeves, shoulders shaking. And dread tangled through it: If the others heard—Carl especially—it wouldn't be forgiven.

For a moment, it was peaceful. Almost warm. As if absurdity itself had bought them a pause.

Then Gwen's eyes fixed on her. "How are you, Mara?"

The question stunned her. No one had asked. Not since the crash.

Mara swallowed hard. "I'm... still here."

Gwen nodded as if that were not only acceptable but important. "That matters."

Silence settled, but not awkward. Grounded. Solid. Mara found herself studying Gwen—composed, breath steady, not prey-like at all.

"You know," Gwen said, voice low, pitched to the needles, "Carly isn't what most people think. Not what you'd call a good person."

Mara stiffened.

"Carl either," Gwen continued, unhurried. "They can be cruel. Not always, but often. You've seen it." Her tone was flat, unbothered, as if cruelty were a plain fact. "They do good things sometimes. Acts that look right. But that's performance."

The words were precise—like a verdict, not a rant.

Mara's chest prickled. She knew some of their history, but Gwen's phrasing hinted at more. What had she endured?

"I don't confuse performance with kindness anymore," Gwen said, softer now. "Can't afford to."

What had Gwen forgiven, again and again?

Gwen looked out toward the storm, breath fogging. "She's my sister. That's part of it. But mostly... I need to give her that chance. To be my sister. Even if she throws it away, I'll know I did my part."

No apology. No weakness. Just conviction, pared to the bone.

Mara's stomach twisted. She had misjudged Gwen completely—not weak, not a hanger-on orbiting Carl and Carly, but a woman with her own compass, choosing the harder path. Stronger than the two she seemed to follow.

When she chose to be that woman. The disconnect clanged in Mara's skull. Where had this woman been hiding?

Through the pine's screen, Carl's voice rose—sharp,

urging them on. Brenna's outline shifted behind him, head shaking.

Mara glanced at Gwen. In the dim green light, her face still held that quiet strength, that strange calm. Then Carly's cough reached them—wet, racking—and Gwen's expression folded. She tightened her hood, rose, and angled toward the others, the mask of service snapping back into place.

Mara stayed crouched, unease pooling cold beneath her coat. Gwen had revealed something here—eloquent, perceptive, steel under softness. Kinder, sharper, and stronger than Mara had ever guessed.

And now she slipped back into the role as though none of it had happened.

Mara shivered, but not from the wind.

If she'd missed this about Gwen Caddell, what else had they been choosing not to see?

The storm gave no answer.

Chapter 28

Mara noticed the posts first: dark stumps jutting from the drift in a straight line.

The trees thinned without warning, trunks parting into a wide white opening. The group stumbled forward and stopped, blinking against the sudden exposure. Wind clawed across the clearing, stronger without branches to break it. That's when she'd seen it.

Stakes. Not scattered or broken like the others they'd passed, but upright and evenly spaced, wire sagging low between them, humming faintly in the gale.

Her chest tightened. "A fence."

The word moved through the group like a spark. Carl's head snapped up, eyes burning through the swelling. Gwen tightened her grip on Carly. Even

Brenna turned fully, hood crusted white, studying the line.

Fences meant fields. Fields meant houses. Houses meant shelter. The logic was ancient.

Carl adjusted Carly by the arm he held, and Gwen did the same. Carly's head lolled against Carl's shoulder, lips blue, breath a fragile whisper. "We follow it," Carl rasped. "It goes somewhere."

Brenna shook her head, snow streaming from her hood. "Could be nothing. The wagon trail is the other way."

"We can't not see where it goes," Gwen whispered. "If there's a chance—"

Carl didn't wait. He bent his head into the storm and stepped out into the open. The others followed, pulled by desperation and by him.

The difference was immediate. Without trees the wind hit them full force, scouring across the crust, flattening drifts, needling their faces raw. Sound that wasn't roar vanished—every breath stripped to fragments. Mara hunched low, arms tight around herself, knee screaming. The cold bit deeper here too. The air itself leeched heat from their bodies.

The fence stretched ahead unbroken. Post after post, each rattling faintly with the tremor of the wire. It felt deliberate—a line laid out to pull them forward.

Minutes blurred.

Carly moaned once—small, as a child in fever—but Carl only gripped her tighter. His legs shuddered with each step, muscles trembling, but he didn't slow. Gwen didn't either.

Then the fence turned—a perfect right angle, vanishing sideways into the storm.

They paused, snow streaming over them, stunned by the geometry. Mara had half believed the fence must lead straight to a farm or road. The angle felt mocking, as if the land had changed its mind.

They followed the second side.

The wind tore at them now, unrelenting. Gwen stumbled, clutching Mara's arm, face raw with cold. Mara felt her knee numb, the pain replaced by a deep, hollow throb that frightened her more. Numbness meant she was losing.

Post by post, the line dragged them forward. Carly coughed, blood flecking Carl's coat. Gwen sobbed once behind her scarf. Brenna's face was unreadable, but her steps faltered.

The next corner came. Another perfect angle. Posts marching off in a clean line.

"Oh no," Gwen whispered.

Carl didn't answer. He bent lower, boots punching holes in the crust, breath ragged. The others followed, unwilling to leave him or Carly, unable to admit the futility clawing at their minds.

By the third side, Mara's legs were lead. The cold sucked at her chest, thinning every breath. Warmth vanished here faster than they could replace it. In the woods, you could trick yourself—branches blocking gusts, your own heat trapped in layers. Out here, the air drank them dry.

She watched the steam of their bodies rise—heat escaping in ghostly threads, torn apart in seconds.

When the final corner came, Mara prayed for a break in the pattern—for a gate, a barn roof, a mailbox, anything.

Instead the posts turned once more, clean as the others.

She remembered reading about trappers or soldiers in the Rockies who mistook one valley for another. They walked themselves in loops until exposure thinned them one by one. Searchers later found their tracks scored over the same path, a white circle of ruin.

She lowered her eyes, watching her boots sink and lift, sink and lift. Mistakes in summer were forgiven. Here, a mistake accumulated until it became death.

When they reached the place where they had started, the line closed. Their own single-file prints met the first post, forming a perfect square cut into the drift.

Nowhere.

They stood in silence. The storm pressed down. The fence rattled faintly.

Carly whimpered again, tiny as a fading ember. Carl bent his head over her, shoulders shaking with a grief he didn't voice.

Mara stared at the shape they'd made—the part she could see, the part she couldn't. Four equal sides. Time wasted. Heat wasted. Carly closer to death for nothing. The geometry felt obscene, as though the land had drawn it through them on purpose.

Brenna turned toward the trees. "We need a windbreak."

Carl didn't speak. He only shifted Carly in his arms and trudged after her, boots dragging. Gwen clutched her sister's limp hand tighter, as she hauled her, eyes fixed on the ground.

Mara stumbled after them, feeling as though part of herself had been left inside that icy square.

A square in the snow.

A band already half erased.

Behind them, the fence rattled on, meaningless, until the storm swallowed its sound.

Chapter 29

The tractor and wagon were still there.

Half buried in snow now, a dismembered carcass pressed deeper into the ditch, boards snapped and ribs jutting like the rib cage of some long-dead thing.

Snow had softened the wreck, blurred its edges, but the wrongness hadn't faded. If anything, the silence around it made it starker.

Mara slowed.

She couldn't help it. It felt like returning to a dream —everything familiar, but bent. The smell had changed too. Less diesel now. More iron. More rot. The wind had peeled drifts back in places, revealing patches of old stain—blood she remembered, half hidden yesterday, half revealed today. Some glittered where cold had crystallized it, frozen rubies scattered across white. Others lay beneath thin sheets of snow, appearing and disappearing with each gust.

Same scene.

Not the same at all.

Animals had found it too. Their tracks circled the stains, looping in curious or nervous spirals. Small ones—foxes, maybe. Others larger. Mara crouched, brushing at a half-filled print. Broad pads. Clear claws. Wolf? Coyote? Either was enough to prick her skin with unease. Another print, half smeared, looked different—bipedal, twisting, almost human.

Or not?

Her mind tried to make meaning of the blur. But one truth held: They had not been alone here.

The relief she'd felt on spotting the trail—the old scar in the woods that meant they weren't lost—curdled quickly. This wasn't a return to safety. It was stepping back into the margin of the map where things had gone wrong.

Someone had sabotaged the trail.

Set the trap.

Killed Willy.

Coming back meant returning to visible teeth.

And the storm had worsened. Of course it had.

Afternoon light was dimming to slate, snow falling thick and endless, pressed sideways by wind that flattened the trees into blurs. Shadows were gone; the world was gray stacked on gray, horizon swallowed entirely. Mara felt the day thinning, bleeding toward night.

Carl looked worse. His eyes were swollen, lids puffed to mismatched purples, one rim slick with a darker bruise. His wrist and hand bulged out of proportion—skin stretched, angry, ungloved now. He must have abandoned the glove; it wouldn't fit anymore, Mara figured. When he touched his head, the motion was stiff and clumsy, like the hand didn't quite belong to him.

And Carly... Carly was slipping fast. Her face was the color of the snow, lips blue, her good hand fluttering weakly against Gwen's. Delirium clouded her gaze. She breathed, shallow and uneven, but she wasn't fighting. Just slumping, compliant in a way that frightened Mara.

She thought—not without guilt—that it was already too late for Carly.

But humans help humans.

Rule one.

Gwen hunched over her sister, arms wrapped tight, cheek pressed to Carly's hair. She wasn't strategizing anymore. She was keeping Carly alive in the simplest way possible: minute by minute. Rocking. Whispering a wordless hum that barely rose above the wind. A lullaby for someone drifting out of reach.

Carly stirred once, muttering nonsense. Gwen kissed her temple, smoothed her hair, tightened her hold.

It was as though she believed pressure alone could keep Carly's soul inside her body.

Brenna stood near the flipped trailer, fingertips tracing iron bolts and splintered boards, gaze flicking toward the sisters with something between pity and calculation—measuring what weight a group could carry. She glanced once at Carl and Mara. Their eyes caught, then slid apart.

"Brenna," Carl called, voice cracking.

She didn't turn.

He tried again, louder. Still nothing. He cursed under his breath. "Doesn't she know her own damn name?"

She had heard him. Mara was sure. It was like the sound slid across her surface without catching. After a long beat, Brenna finally looked up and nodded once, her voice low but steady: Carly wasn't in good shape. They couldn't risk the march back.

The storm did not relent.

For a moment, Mara felt like they stood inside a snow globe—every flurry suspended, swirling, erasing, beautiful and suffocating all at once. A reminder: stand still long enough and even the memory of you disappears.

Carly was vanishing fastest. The storm wasn't just erasing their tracks. It was erasing Carly.

The sky lowered, the air colder than the afternoon

before. Someone in their circle was dying. All of them were injured, battered, half frozen. Willy's last fire starter was all they had left.

They would burn it here.

They worked quickly.

Carl dragged branches into a crooked pile; Mara helped where she could, her knee sharp and loose. Brenna shoveled and packed snow into a ring, shoulders rigid with purpose. She pulled a plank from the trailer, laid a blanket across it, making a rough platform for Mara and herself. Another platform for Carl, Gwen, and Carly—angled so they could sit sheltered between the fire and the overturned wagon. Fire in front, wreck at their backs. A thin pocket carved from storm and ruin.

Mara couldn't shake the dissonance. Building shelter at the site of the trap. Using the wreck that had nearly killed them as their shield. It felt sacrilegious and yet inevitable. Shelter was shelter. Fire was fire.

If the wreck remembered them, it stayed silent.

Carl stacked branches into a crooked cone. His swollen hand jerked with every movement. Willy's last fire starter slid beneath the pile, struck fast.

Sparks spat, then flared.

The flame burned bright and oily—too confident at first. Rushed, Mara thought. He hadn't chosen the right wood, only grabbed whatever he could.

She and Brenna crouched in, pulling bark from the

thinner sticks. The bark clung wet, stringy, smelling of rot. Each strip came away damp. They fed the peeled lengths to the fire. The starter seized them, but the sticks hissed sharply, protesting, smoke rising in thick white plumes.

Brenna brushed snow from another branch. Her glove came away wet. She shot Mara a look: *This isn't good fuel.* Mara nodded. The wood would smolder, spit water, collapse into mush. It would burn out before it warmed them.

Still they worked—scraping bark, breaking sticks, feeding the reluctant flame. The fire starter forced the pile alive, but the branches sagged black at the edges, smoking more than they burned. Each hiss sounded like steam forced from a wound.

Mara's eyes drifted to the wreck. Splintered ribs of the flatbed jutted pale from the drift. She ran her glove over one as she pulled it free, brushing snow loose. Processed lumber. Harder grain. It might burn cleaner. It might last. She dragged a piece back and set it near the hissing pile.

The fire caught in bursts, then faltered, like a chest struggling for air. It reminded her too much of Carly— flickering, forced forward only by their hands. Each hiss of wet wood was like Carly's cough. Each moment of flame like her pulse.

Brenna coughed through the smoke, fed a drier

branch into Carl's pyramid. The flame licked, then sulked.

Still, Mara marveled at how quickly they had formed this tiny world. Humans helping humans. A crude wall against the wind. A ring to hold heat. A chance for one more night.

Fragile, temporary.

But theirs.

The storm swelled around them, pressing down like a weight. Day bled away, swallowed by the blizzard. Yet inside their crooked circle, a glow flickered—weak, hissing, acrid, but enough.

This was where they would weather the storm.

Where they would try to save Carly.

Where they would try to save each other.

Mara couldn't help but sense that they had already failed.

Chapter 30

The fire burned, but not right. Mara felt it before she studied it. Carl had rushed, stacking branches with clumsy, swollen hands. The starter flared bright, but the wood only smoldered. It hissed, spat water, smoked like green pine. Heat came thin, fragile. Wrong.

Carl crouched close, fumbling through Willy's satchel. He pulled out a dented can of vegetables. A ritual, Mara realized—Willy had done this before. Survival made ceremony of scraps.

Carl drew the knife, tried venting the can, and gasped. The blade slipped, slicing the palm he'd already injured. Blood welled instantly. He swore, pressed the cut to his coat, and kept working until a jagged opening gave. He set the can on a flat stone at the fire's edge.

They didn't wait long. The contents weren't hot, not

cold either. Warm enough for a body in crisis. Carl coaxed a spoonful past Carly's lips, swallowed one himself, then handed it to Mara.

The tin rim burned her cracked hands. The taste was brine and metal, but hunger made it almost sweet. She swallowed gratefully and passed it to Brenna.

The circle continued. Five figures huddled in snow and shadow, sharing meager food the way countless had before them. Not enough to fill. Just enough to prove they were still alive.

The overturned wagon loomed at their backs, the fire at their front. Mara pressed closer. The cold behind her bit no less than the night before, but the illusion of shelter mattered. The wreck caught the fire's breath and ghosted it back at them.

The flames hissed, fighting wet fuel. The storm leaned in. Carly moaned faintly in Gwen's arms, lips blue, body slack. Gwen rocked her, cheek in her hair, humming wordless comfort.

They were alive. Barely.

Carl stared into the flames, eyes hollowed out. His voice cracked low, meant for Gwen but heard by all: "We weren't even supposed to be here."

The words carried history. Blame. A wound reopened.

Gwen flinched but said nothing. Carly's gaze drifted, unfixed.

Mara felt pity stir. Gwen wasn't radiant like Brenna —not a beacon—but there was something enduring in her, a quiet depth that had carried too much and kept going. A steadiness surfaced in her now, sharp and unexpected. Mara realized she had been looking at one kind of woman and was suddenly seeing another beneath.

But still her eyes slid back to Brenna. Always Brenna. Even frostbitten, lashes iced stiff, her chin lifted with pride. In the firelight, her irises flashed like coins. Mara hated how her gaze kept slipping there.

She forced herself to scan the circle. One dead already—Willy. Carly sliding fast. The rest battered, limping, ribs bruised, wrists swollen, skin raw with cold. By any measure, they were wrecks. Yet here they were, huddled again around a fire spitting weak light. Hope was thin, but it was hope. The warmth on her face, bodies pressed close—it startled her with its comfort. As if some ancient law applied: Pain plus people equaled safety, however fleeting.

That was when Carl said it, flat as naming weather: "We're all gonna die out here."

The words hit like weight.

Brenna's lips parted, then shut. Chin tilted. Defiant, but not denying.

Gwen clutched Carly closer. Her voice—almost a hum: "We're all gonna die out here." Softer. Slower. As if spoken from beneath the snow.

The circle stilled. The fire popped. Mara's pulse quickened.

Death. Likely, yes. Certain, no.

And then the thought slipped out of her, barely louder than breath: "I'm having the *thought* that we're all going to die..."

Her voice cracked. The others noticed.

Gwen's head lifted slowly, eyes widening slightly, wet, sharp as knives. "What did you just say?"

Mara blinked. Gestured weakly back toward Carl and Gwen. "Just... agreeing. We're in trouble."

Gwen shook her head. "Not that. The way you said it. That phrase."

"I'm having the thought that we're going to die," Mara repeated, uneasy.

Gwen's voice dropped, soft, almost reverent. "That's something Dr. Hill would say."

The name split the air.

Brenna flinched. Small, but unmistakable. Her shoulders tightened. Her hands froze on her knees.

Mara caught the shift. Gwen saw it too.

"Brenna?"

Brenna blinked, swallowed. "Dr. Gregory Hill?"

Gwen nodded once. Small. Certain.

Brenna's face crumpled. "I saw him. In Michigan. Years ago. After I... lost someone. The closest person I had. The only person." The words fell out, raw. "I was in the worst place. He helped. More than anyone ever had. But I stopped going. I couldn't keep it up." She shook her head, pleading. "I don't understand how *you* could know him, Gwen. What are the odds?"

Snow hissed against the fire, steam rising thinly. Eyes turned to Mara.

She nodded. "Panic disorder. I've been seeing him too."

Silence thickened. Then Gwen lifted her head. Her voice steadied, cutting clean through the storm.

"Would you like to know," she said, "what I saw Dr. Hill for?"

No one breathed. Carl's eyes flickered, guilt trembling behind them.

"My immune system attacked my nerves," Gwen said. "Guillain-Barré. I was too weak to walk. Too weak to get up. Too weak to make it to the bathroom. And when I couldn't—when I had accidents—they left me in it. Days at a time. Sitting in my own filth."

"Gwen—" Carl muttered, but she cut him off.

"In the hospital, they were attentive enough. But once I came home... not a week passed before Mom died." Her voice tightened.

Carl's jaw locked. Gwen continued.

"The day of her wake, I'd wet myself in my chair. Family still around. Carly made a show of it—squeezing my shoulder, performing sympathy. Then she rolled me to my room and left me. Never changed me. Never checked. I crawled out of that chair myself. Dragged myself to the bed. Stripped my soaked pants. Slid under sheets that weren't clean, but at least were dry."

Her mouth trembled, but the voice stayed steady.

"Later I lost control again. Lay in it. Begging. Carly stood in the doorway and told me if I didn't stop whining, she'd leave me longer. Then she said they needed space. And that's when she and Carl wheeled the casket in."

Carl twitched, half rising before collapsing back.

A sharp pop from the fire cracked through the circle, sparks leaping. Mara flinched—not from fear but from being torn out of Gwen's story. She realized she'd been holding her breath, the world narrowed to the flame and Gwen's voice. The fire snapped back at her; the storm returned, gnawing at them again.

"And when the house went quiet," Gwen said, "Carl came. Drunk. Carly giggling in the hall. He flicked the light on, grinning, and *opened the casket*. I stared at Mom's face—gray, waxed—inches from mine. Then he shut the light off. Left me in the dark with her."

Her lips pressed thin.

"I'm a mom. Did you know that? When my son was small, even the word *potty* felt poisoned. Something every parent says a thousand times—they'd already made it rancid. Tainted it. Stolen it."

She paused, breath hitching.

"The morning after the wake, *before* they cleaned me, do you know what they brought me? A gas-station tuna sandwich. And a dill pickle. I gagged. They saw. So the next day—and the next—tuna sandwich. Pickle. Until I couldn't even look at either without tasting piss and rot."

Her hands tightened on Carly's limp arm.

"When my strength returned, they got angry. Meals stopped. They'd set plates just inside the room and wait for me to crawl. Once, I didn't reach it fast enough, and Carly laughed. Told me I must not be hungry."

Her gaze cut directly to Carl.

Mara felt something inside her shift—a plate sliding under the earth. She had misread Gwen. Fragile? Passive? No. Watching her now—composed, lucid, unblinking as she dragged their ugliness into the firelight —Mara saw a spine of iron.

Gwen wasn't broken. She was the anchor, or could be if she chose it. She'd brought Carl and Carly here, not as weight but as witness: to test whether family could survive truth.

"When I was back on my feet," Gwen said softly, "the shame clung. Nights wet. Meetings torture. Every laugh in a room felt aimed at me. It took years to pretend I was human again. For all of it, I have Carly and Carl to thank—the caretakers. The saviors."

The storm rattled the wreck, spraying snow across their boots.

Gwen exhaled. "I told myself I was over it. That surviving something like this might burn the rest out. Maybe Dr. Hill was right—maybe exposure could cure fear."

Mara sat transfixed. Gwen's words hung in the cold like stones. And her own eyes drifted—inevitably—back to Brenna. Lashes wet. Firelight gold in her pupils.

The air felt charged, corrupted—like before a tornado. The Dr. Hill connection wasn't coincidence. It was too exact. Too impossible. All of them threaded by the same man's words.

Even the fire seemed to pause. The hiss softened. The storm muted. As if the world itself had stopped to listen.

To witness.

Then a gust tore through the wreck, scattering sparks. Mara shivered, not just from cold. They were bound now—by hunger, wounds, the storm, and by the strange, impossible non-coincidence of the same man shaping each of their shadows.

She pressed closer to the fire, its warmth thin but all they had.

And Mara felt certain, in that moment, that the hollow was preparing to consume them.

Chapter 31

The fire was dying.

Not just low—distorted. Coals buried under slush hissed weakly, coughing steam instead of heat. Smoke rose in shreds before the wind tore it apart. What little glow remained wasn't light so much as a faint ember stain on their faces, as though they sat around the ghost of a hearth.

The storm pressed in with endurance to claim the circle. Drifts leaned higher against their backs, filling their footprints as they sat.

Behind them, Carly stirred. A gurgling rasp broke from her throat, wet and uneven, followed by a thin moan that sagged into silence. She was still clinging when her body should have been done.

In the ember glow, Carl's face looked wrong. Both eyes swollen purple, lids puffed to slits, the bruises catching the firelight in a way that hollowed him, carving shadows until he seemed more mask than man.

Mara knew it was a trick of light, but the sight chilled her—as though the woods were sculpting him into something no longer human.

The fire didn't want them anymore. And in its coughing, sputtering ruin, Mara saw Carly mirrored—warmth failing, smoke where breath should be, a body collapsing despite every hand trying to coax it back.

She leaned into Brenna, close enough to feel her shoulder under the quilts. Their breaths mingled in faint clouds rising into a sky that seemed lower now—heavy, oppressive.

Then the sound again.

Not the fire. Not the storm.

Carly.

Retching—thin at first, then violent, her body folding and unfolding in Gwen's arms. Vomit spattered blankets, then bile, then threads of red so dark they looked black.

Her broken finger jerked stiffly at the air. Gwen tried to hold her, whispering reassurances that vanished into the noise. Carl lurched closer, one hand pressed to his ruined eye, the other hovering as though afraid to touch his wife.

The retching went on, and Mara's own stomach didn't lurch the way it should have.

That unsettled her.

She thought of Dr. Hill—how he'd once talked about vomiting as a primal alarm bell, a survival signal meant to protect the tribe. Bodies teaching each other what was safe.

She thought of herself, sick at the sight of Willy. Brenna too. Panic sickness. Shock sickness. Reflexes trying to keep them alive.

But Carly? This felt different.

Hypothermia didn't do this. Hypothermia was a quiet thief; it slowed, silenced, stilled. It didn't tear the body with spasms or force vomiting again and again.

Then what was it?

Food poisoning made no sense—they'd all shared the can. Poison? Carly was already half dead. Overkill, if intentional.

Or maybe it was something already inside her—a rot waiting for its moment. Maybe it was her stubbornness, the sheer fact she'd lasted this long, the rage of a human body unwilling to die.

Mara wasn't sure which thought was worse.

The sounds dwindled. Retching collapsed into shallow gasps, then silence. Gwen's humming frayed into sobs. Carl pressed his forehead to Carly's shoulder, lips moving in denial.

The fire guttered to almost nothing. No hiss. No smoke. Only a half glow in blackened wood half buried under new snow. Their hard-won shelter was dissolving back into white.

Shapes into shadow.

Even the soft glow the storm had reflected earlier seemed gone, as though the night itself had stolen it. Clouds pressed low, smothering what little luminescence remained. Mara blinked, but the dark held. The world was blind. Only a faint rim of white edged her vision.

Brenna's hand slipped into hers—cold, trembling.

Mara pulled her closer, pressed their foreheads together, felt frost clinging to Brenna's lashes. Brenna let out a thin sob, then quieted.

Mara wrapped her arms around her—half comfort, half survival. She couldn't tell them apart anymore. She wasn't sure she wanted to. The question stung: Was Brenna offering this because she wanted Mara, or because she knew Mara needed it? The thought pricked like ice, sharp and unresolved.

Across the ruins of their circle, Gwen rocked Carly's dead or nearly dead body, keening low. Carl crouched beside them, swollen eyes dark and ruined.

Two dead. Four left.

Or three and a ghost.

Mara shut her eyes. Her head pounded, her knee screamed when she shifted, and cold gnawed mercilessly into damp blankets. Sleep whispered at her—sly, coaxing. Hypothermia's hand: Just close your eyes. Rest. It will be easier. She thought in the voice of Dr. Hill again: Don't sleep. Not in the cold.

But she was so tired.

Her thoughts drifted around the group—this collection of battered, unraveling humans pulled together by storm and disaster. She nearly called them friends, but the word felt alive in a way none of them were anymore. Still, they had tried. For Carly. For each other. Humans helping humans, knowing full well it might not be enough.

She hoped she had been reliable. For Gwen, who deserved protection. For Brenna, whose nearness she'd longed for since they'd met. Even for Carl and Carly, as cruel as they had been.

They had all tried.

The dark tightened around them. Breath rose white and vanished. Brenna inched closer—shoulder to shoulder, then hip to hip—until without speaking they lay side by side under the wool blankets, bodies pressed into one line. Rolled tight like carpet, sharing heat because there was no other way.

Mara could hardly believe it. Days of watching Brenna from across fires and storms, wanting her warmth, aching for her presence—and now here she was, not just close but holding her. It felt illicit with Carly's now deceased body still warm nearby, but Mara couldn't stop the flush of relief.

Like stealing from the dead.

But she didn't care.

Sleep came.

She had chased it for years—stared at ceilings, begged for it, never caught it. And now, when she needed to stay awake most, it arrived willingly.

Gentle.

Courteous.

Like a lover easing her in with a hand at her back.

She knew the truth. Do not fall asleep in the snow. In the cold. But the lure was soft, irresistible.

She didn't resist.

The storm pressed its hand over the camp.

And Mara slept.

Chapter 32

Dr. Hill:

You said last week felt better. Tell me more about that.

Mara:

Better in that I could breathe. That sounds cliché, but that's how it felt. A breather. No exposure homework, no planning my day around what I agreed to confront.

Dr. Hill:

So the pause was useful.

Mara:

Very. I didn't realize how much
pressure it put on me until it was
gone. It's like walking with a
backpack you think is part of your
body. Then someone takes it off,
and you realize you'd been bent
double the whole time.

Dr. Hill:

That's a strong image. What did
you notice about yourself without
the backpack?

Mara:

That I wasn't constantly bracing. I
could actually look around. I even
did small things—sat in a café
without headphones, tried a
different bus route. Not dramatic,
but not homework either. I wanted
to build the experiment myself.
To try.

Dr. Hill:

And how did it feel?

Mara:

Like the world didn't collapse. I
was uncomfortable, sure. My
heart raced. But nothing
happened. No one laughed, no
one pointed. I was just… alive,
anxious, but alive. And I chose it.

Dr. Hill:

Which tells you what?

> **Mara:**
>
> That maybe my fear isn't a
> prophecy. It's just a fear.

Dr. Hill:

Let's stay with that. Fear of what?

> **Mara:**
>
> Of death. Always, at the root, it's
> that. That panic means dying, that
> embarrassment means dying, that
> being alone means dying. It
> always circles back.

Dr. Hill:

How long has death been this
present for you?

> **Mara:**
>
> As far back as I can remember. I'd
> hear about someone collapsing in
> a store or on the news, and I'd
> think, that'll be me. At night I'd
> feel my heart and think it was
> about to stop.

Dr. Hill:

What is it like when those
thoughts come?

Mara:

It's like the air changes. Heavy,
charged. I imagine people finding
me, or worse, not finding me. My
body being discovered after days.
Sometimes I picture the funeral —
who would even come.
Sometimes no one.

Dr. Hill:

What do you notice about that
image?

Mara:

It's not even the dying. It's being
forgotten. Being meaningless.
Like I was a shadow that never
left a mark.

Dr. Hill:

That brings me to an exercise.
Three words for your tombstone.
If you're willing.

Mara:

We've done this before.

Dr. Hill:

Humor me.

Mara:

Merciful. Loyal. Watchful.

Dr. Hill:

That's not a set I hear often. Tell
me about merciful.

Mara:

Mercy feels close to compassion, but deeper—easing what's unbearable so someone doesn't carry it alone. If I can make life lighter, then I mattered.

Dr. Hill:

Watchful you've spoken of before.

Mara:

Because I'm always observing. I notice tone shifts, expressions, the way a room feels. I can't turn it off, but I think it's also how I protect myself.

Dr. Hill:

And loyal?

Mara:

Loyalty is staying when it would be easier to leave. I need that. To stay tethered.

Dr. Hill:

Tethered to what?

Mara:

To what's right. To the bond between people. Even when it doesn't feel good. Even when it hurts.

Dr. Hill:

You see loyalty as crucial.

Mara:

Yes. Fear says, look out for
yourself. Cut loose. Loyalty says
you stay. You don't abandon. You
don't betray what's keeping
everyone together.

Dr. Hill:

That sounds close to another
word you didn't choose.

Mara:

Family.

Mara:

I almost put it on my list. But
"family" can mean blood, or
obligation, or the people who hurt
you most. I didn't want that tangle
carved on my stone.

Chapter 33

Mara woke to warmth that wasn't there.

For a moment, with her eyes still closed, she knew she'd been pressed against Brenna all night. The memory clung to her skin in tingles: a pocket of shared heat, the faint weight of an arm across her ribs. It lingered like an afterimage of safety, a body-shaped echo she wanted to reach for. But when she stretched her hand into the hollow, there was nothing. Only cold.

She opened her eyes slowly, bracing for the same gray walls of snow and wind that had battered them for days.

But the world had shifted.

The air on her face felt softer—still cold, yes, but not the murderous kind that cut straight to bone. She drew a long breath, and it didn't tear at her lungs. Above her, the sky had brightened into a wide, hard gray-blue, clouds scattered thinly across it. No flakes fell. The wind, that constant razored hand, had eased into sporadic breaths.

It was still winter, but it was no longer war.

The hush unsettled her almost as much as the blizzard had. Storms carried sound; they roared, explained their violence. This silence felt stranger—like a stage stripped bare after the actors had gone. Even the birds were absent. No wingbeat, no call. Just snow heaped heavy on branches, an occasional plop of meltwater, air so still it seemed to be listening.

Hope hit her hard enough to tighten her throat. If the storm had truly broken, then surely help wasn't far. Search parties. Cleared roads. Rescue made possible again.

This morning didn't feel like death. It felt like reprieve. She nearly smiled. *Damn. It's almost pleasant.*

Her gaze drifted over their makeshift camp. Inches of snow had swallowed everything they'd built. The wind wall slouched like a tired spine. Blankets were frosted stiff. Footprints they had carved and retraced were filled. Their little fortress looked half buried, as though it, too, had slept.

And then she saw Carly.

The hope drained clean.

Carly lay flat, white as the drifts framing her. Arms

flung wide, legs splayed, her shape pressed into the snow like some obscene snow angel. Her mouth sagged half open, blood dried at the corners, vomit crusted along her chin and chest. The finger broken in the crash jutted upward, frozen in a crooked salute. Her eyes, open and glassy, stared at the bright sky that had arrived too late.

Mara's chest ached. She had known, of course—had heard Carly's breathing grow wet, seen the retching, the shuddering fits, the blood. She'd known there was no return from that slope. And still the sight tore at her, as if death had waited for daylight to show its work.

She couldn't believe she had slept.

Slept through the fire collapsing to ash. Slept through the final moments of Carly seizing and expelling her own life. Slept through the quiet of someone leaving the world. Her body had stolen rest while someone just feet away was dead or dying.

A compulsion seized her then: She had to close those eyes. Carly was gone, yes, but she had been one of them. One of the circle. They had shared fire, food, breath. That meant something. Even dead, she deserved care.

Mara shifted to her knees. Pain answered.

A jolt seared from her knee up to behind her right ear, sharp as an axe splitting wood. Her vision pinwheeled dark, the world tightening and expanding. Her knee stabbed with a wrongness that nearly folded her.

She froze, panting, nausea cresting.

Then she crawled.

Each drag forward drove pain through her skull. Dried blood tugged at her scalp. Bile crept up her throat. Her knee ground like a hinge kicked sideways. She was starving, thirsty, limbs heavy as sandbags. Her arms shook, elbows skidding in the snow as she hauled herself toward the body.

By the time she reached Carly, she was trembling so hard she nearly collapsed on top of her. She forced herself upright, hunched and gasping beside the dead woman.

Close the eyes. She reached with clumsy fingers, pressing the lids down. They resisted, stiff with frost. When they finally slipped shut, they popped back open —snapping skyward again.

Mara jerked her hand away, face flushing hot with shame. Of course. Bodies froze this way. Still, she tried once more, gentle, holding. But the lids rolled back again, as if on invisible wires.

Carly stared blankly upward.

Unblinking. Unreachable.

Mara sagged, trembling. Exhaustion flooded her— not just from the crawl or the pain but from the grief itself. It weighed heavier than the snow.

But the storm had passed.

And that was when she noticed the other silence.

She lifted her head. Across the camp, Carl and Brenna faced one another. They didn't speak, but the air between them was jagged as shattered glass.

Carl looked wrecked—red-eyed, jaw clenched so tight it trembled. Grief poured off him in waves, channeled into a fury that seemed to hold him upright. He looked like he hadn't moved in hours. Just glaring, bleeding disdain without sound.

Brenna met it with stillness. Confidence. Her face, beautiful even now, had hardened into something sharp. She leaned forward slightly, eyes unflinching. No apology. No fear.

The storm might have passed, but something colder had settled between them.

Mara's pulse climbed. *This is worse than the storm.*

And then she remembered how far they had come. Willy gone. Now Carly. Gwen battered. Carl half blind, hands swollen. Herself broken open in places she didn't know could crack.

But through it all, they had stuck together. Tried.

Humans helping humans—it had meant something.

A movement caught her eye.

Gwen.

She was kneeling beside Carly's body, not weeping now, but focused. Her fingers hovered, then reached for the gloves at her dead sister's side—Mara's gloves, the pair she had pressed into Carly's hands after the group had found her. Gwen slid them on herself with care, but clumsy over trembling fingers.

When she looked up, her eyes met Mara's. For a breath, her lips tugged into something faint but genuine. A thank-you. A recognition. It landed in Mara's chest like modest warmth. But also betrayal.

Then Gwen stood.

Turned.

And began walking away.

Not toward Carl. Not toward Brenna. Not toward any of them. Her posture held no stumble, no sway of exhaustion at this moment. It wasn't the body of someone unraveling but of someone decided.

Each step deliberate, back unbent, head high—as though walking into a future only she could see.

Mara felt the distinction like a blade: Gwen wasn't failing. She was choosing. Choosing distance. Choosing to step out of their circle. Abandonment not as accident but as verdict.

Gwen moved down the trail, then off into the woods, away from the wreck, away from them.

Towards the cave.

Her back straight. Steps slow but certain.

Mara's stomach dropped. The air thickened, as if everyone understood at once.

She's leaving us.

Her gaze whipped back to Carl.

That was when she saw the root in his hand.

Small, cream-colored, knobs smooth, faint threads of gold beneath the skin. Innocent-looking.

Almost like food.

When he spoke, his voice was a breaking branch in frost.

"I know what water hemlock is, Brenna."

Hemlock.

Mara knew the word from somewhere—Socrates, maybe, the poisoned cup. She had never imagined it as something you could hold. A root pulled from the earth. A thing you could feed someone.

And in that instant it aligned. Carl wasn't just clutching a plant. He was holding an answer.

In his mind, Brenna hadn't been unlucky. She hadn't been careless. She had killed.

She had slipped poison into Carly's body—maybe into all of theirs when they shared that can of vegetables the night before.

His silence, his stiffness, his grief—narrowing now, hardening to blame.

Carl's voice cracked the air.

"You poisoned my fucking wife."

Chapter 34

Mara felt it in her bones: A verdict had been spoken. Nothing that came after would belong to the same circle of people who had shared fire the night before.

The storm had cleared. The sky promised reprieve, rescue, life. And yet here, on this trail, they were not saved. They were finally breaking. Mara cringed at the irony. *Leave it to humans,* she thought, *to survive the storm only to rip each other apart the moment the weather permitted.*

Her chest tightened as she mentally recited their storm's casualties. Willy—gone. Carly—gone. Gwen—who had met her eyes with that faint, insufficient gratitude before walking down the trail alone. And Brenna—whose body Mara had clung to through the night—now stood squared off against Carl like a stranger.

She wanted to believe survival had bound them. Wanted it desperately. But the scene before her said otherwise.

Her gaze drifted to the snow between them. That was when she saw it: Willy's satchel, slumped near Carly's outstretched hand. And beside it, his long knife in its sheath. The holster was rough brown leather, worn dark by years of use, the flap snapped shut. Faint smears of red traced the holster's stitched seam—blood she hadn't noticed before.

She reached for it without thinking. The leather met her palm warm, softened by wear. She gripped it hard, clutching the coarse surface as though the knife inside could steady her. Absurd comfort. A thing made to cut and bleed had become her anchor—

Like its owner before it.

More than that, the knife felt honest.

It didn't pretend. It cut, or it didn't.

That was order. That was continuity. And it stung bitterly that the one man who had built, who had led, was gone—while those remaining were arming themselves with roots and branches, reverting to the oldest kind of violence.

Her eyes lifted again. Brenna.

Quiet Brenna, who had always moved at the edge of the circle. Now she stood with a length of wood in her hands—three feet long, thicker at one end, narrowing to a blunt point. A stripped branch, wielded like a club.

For a split second, Mara almost laughed; it was cartoonish, a caveman sketch. But the absurdity curdled quickly.

That was the oldest weapon there was.

One of, anyway.

Humans had killed with less since the beginning.

And Brenna did not look timid now. She looked alive in a way that chilled Mara more than the storm had. Eyes narrowed. Shoulders squared. Carl was seeing her clearly for the first time—the real Brenna. Not the distant one they'd been introduced to. Something older. Sharper.

A survivor.

Up close.

Mara's pulse quickened. She gripped the knife sheath as though it alone tied her to the earth.

Carl raised his hand. The root gleamed pale in his fist—knotted, innocent-looking. Water hemlock. Mara had known it only as a story of poison. Yet here it was, in the hand of a grieving man, proof in his mind that the woman across from him hadn't just failed to save Carly— she had killed her.

A bit of root, dropped into their shared can. Just in time for Carly's turn.

"You poisoned her," Carl said again, his voice snapping like frozen wood.

That was it.

The circle was broken.

The air felt brittle, ready to splinter. Neither lunged, but Mara heard the not-faint crunch of snow—one or both shifting, bracing. Brenna's face tightened, and to Mara's shock, a grin crept in.

Not fear.

Not apology.

Something colder: vengeance, joy. And Carl—whom Gwen had once hinted could be cruel behind closed doors—looked utterly unmasked now. Fury, bare and seething, as if he'd spent years waiting for permission to hurt someone.

These people, Mara thought, *don't protect each other anymore. They don't belong to each other.*

The tribe had broken.

She moved before she could think.

Knife sheathed in her grip, she bolted down the trail. Snow clutched at her boots. Branches whipped her arms. Her lungs burned icy, her breath ragged. The path pitched away beneath her, legs stumbling to keep pace with her panic.

Her foot caught on something unseen. She pitched forward, knee slamming into drift. The snow gave with a muffled crunch, but beneath her palm, something harder pressed through—a lattice.

She tore at it. Sticks snapped under her hands, the grid jerking back to reveal what lay beneath: sharpened stakes, their tips black with rot. Rusted barbed wire coiled like snakes. And farther down, heavy plow blades, iron edges bright and cruelly tended.

A pit—deliberate, waiting.

Her stomach lurched.

Fuck.

The woods had teeth. Not wolves, not weather—human teeth. Set carefully, covered over, hidden by snow. And the way the drifts curled to conceal it, the way the wind had smoothed the false ground, made it feel less like a trap in the forest and more like something the forest itself had grown.

Complicit.

Eager.

She spun, scanning every drift, every hollow. If there was one trap, there could be dozens. Even the silence felt sharpened, each gust a blade across her skin.

A thought slashed through her: Gwen had walked away. And Mara could have. Mara made the right choice staying. Even if for just those few moments more. To not be the first to leave.

She staggered upright and pushed on, heart hammering loud enough to drown the wind.

The trail forked around a clutch of pines. Mara ducked into the crook, crouching low with her back against the trunks. Snow bit through her pants, but she didn't move. Couldn't. Every muscle shivered with the effort of stillness.

Then came the sound.

Boots.

Pounding.

Relentless.

A figure burst onto the trail she had fled—breath ragged, limbs jerking. Too far for features. Only frantic motion, wrong and desperate.

Closer.

Faster.

Mara's pulse lashed. They were coming straight for her. If it was Carl, he was armed with grief and rage. If Brenna—then wood in her hands and a sharpened quiet in her eyes.

Either way, death wore a human face now.

Her body trembled too hard to rise. Her mind screamed to move, shout, do anything.

And then the thought hit: *They hadn't seen the pit.*

Her throat clenched. The warning strangled before it rose. Dr. Hill's voice flickered through her mind—calm, maddening: *Humans help humans.* It had sounded simple in therapy. Now it sounded like a sentence.

She hesitated—just a heartbeat. Fear demanded silence. Principle demanded voice.

The words tore out, ragged and raw. "Stop!"

The figure's head snapped toward her, hesitation flashing—and then they ran faster, boots hammering straight down the center of the trail.

The false ground gave way.

Wood cracked. Snow collapsed.

The figure vanished with a sound that split the forest. Impact followed in layers: sticks breaking like bones, wire shrieking against flesh, and finally the blunt, sick thud of body on steel.

Silence returned, heavier than before.

Then—from below—a sound seeped up. Wet. Guttural. Stubborn.

Not words.

Not quite life.

Something in between.

Mara staggered toward the pit, horror clawing at her ribs.

"Humans help humans," she whispered—no longer sure whose voice it was.

Chapter 35

The pit gaped beneath her like a wound in the earth. The body sprawled among spools of wire and sharpened sticks looked already dead —face-down, motionless, dark blood soaking into snow.

Carl's jacket was torn wide where a stake jutted from his left shoulder blade, angled shallow—more hook than spear.

She stared at the back of his head, hair matted stiff with more blood.

Then the body twitched. A hand clawed weakly at the wire, barbs pinging against themselves and him.

"Mara..." His voice was hoarse, ragged—clear enough to freeze her. He was alive. And conscious. Somehow, he knew she was there.

He lifted his head just enough for her to see the ruin of his face. Both eyes were swollen purple, nearly sealed, lids puffed as though the storm had beaten him from the inside out. His lips trembled, skin gray with shock.

One bloodshot eye rolled toward her and fixed.

"Mara. Please."

Above the pit, the woods were almost serene. The storm had passed. Blue-gray sky glittered through branches—clean. Peaceful.

But here, in this gouged earth under that gentle sky, the violence sharpened in the quiet. As if the land had softened only to make room for this.

Her boots scraped the rim. To stay above meant letting him die alone below. To go down meant stepping into the wire, the blood, the wreckage of Carl.

She lowered herself down.

Carl turned toward her with slow, agonized motion, his puffed eyes straining open. His groan shuddered through her chest.

She dropped in fully. Barbs tore at her sleeves, snow collapsing around them. The air down here was wet, iron-thick, sharp enough to sting her sinuses.

She forced herself to face him.

The sight folded her stomach. His gaze swam—glassy, desperate—purpled lids fluttering. He clutched at her sleeve, smearing blood down her arm.

"You have to," he rasped. "Get me off it. I can't stay. Brenna's going to kill me."

Mara shook her head, bile rising.

"Now." His body convulsed, a raw groan tearing loose. "*Now!*"

She braced her shoulder against his ribs, locked her arms around him—a grotesque embrace—and pushed him up and off the stake.

The stake tore partially free with a wet, sucking grind.

Carl screamed, a breaking wail that made her vision spark. He collapsed against her.

Silent.

She froze—terrified she had killed him. His head lolled against her cheek, warmth of fresh blood slicking her skin. Then his chest hitched. A wet gasp. His eyes flickered open, wild behind swelling.

"You can't stop," he sobbed. "No matter what. Please."

She swallowed hard. Set herself again. Pressed close. Drove upward.

Up and off.

Another cry tore the air open. Blood gushed hot down her arms as the wood slid free.

By the time she dragged him off the stake, they were tangled in wire, their clothes shredded, her hands slick with blood. Carl sagged, sobbing, then slumped motionless against the earthen wall.

She hooked her arms under his shoulders and hauled. Muscles screaming, she clawed them both, him first, upward until they spilled onto the churned snow above the pit.

For a beat, stillness.

Then Carl writhed, clutching his stomach. His purpled eyes fluttered, his body twitching. A thin keening leaked from him—half breath, half pain.

Humans help humans, she thought. But her legs already knew the truth as she stood.

A sound snapped her head up.

Down the trail, snow blowing between trees, a figure trudged closer. Still far, but unmistakable.

Brenna.

Mara swore she saw her eyes flash toward her.

Mara looked at Carl. Blood soaked his jacket. His arms clutched his belly. His swollen face twisted not with pleading now but confusion—bewildered he was still here, bewildered she was still standing over him.

She couldn't drag him. Couldn't shield him. Could hardly stand, her clothes drenched with his blood.

The math was brutal: He was finished. Helping him meant dying with him.

Her chest wanted to kneel. Her legs moved. A jog at first, each step away a verdict—betrayal made flesh. *Principles are for people who have choices*, she thought.

Through the trees, fifty yards off, she saw Gwen. Moving parallel, deeper into the woods. Her figure was small against the drifts, deliberate, unbent, like a ghost choosing its own path.

Their eyes met—brief recognition, almost relief. Mara lifted a hand. Weak. Hopeful.

Gwen only shook her head, faint but firm, gaze unreadable. Then turned away. A choice, not collapse. She had decided, and she was not coming back. Something cracked in Mara then, colder than the air.

A new sound shifted the world—the crunch of snow, the rasp of breath.

Carl.

He didn't stand; he unfolded, dragged upright by panic. Swaying. Facing Mara like a man lost in the woods. His body still running commands his mind had already lost. He trudged forward as though his body had forgotten the law of injury.

Behind him came Brenna.

She carried the heavy branch in both hands, stripped smooth. Her grip was locked. Her face twisted in a fierce, gleeful fury—justice and rage fused, both judge and executioner.

Mara froze. Gwen did too.

They saw the first blow before they heard it.

The branch smashed the back of Carl's head, hair puffing grotesquely forward as though his skull had ballooned and collapsed. Then the sound arrived—a crack sharp as gunfire.

Carl staggered.

Somehow did not fall. He pitched forward, caught himself, stumbled in blind steps.

The second blow dropped him.

Brenna struck again. And again. Each swing brutal, rhythmic. A cadence.

Gwen turned and ran. Mara ran too.

Behind them, the violence continued—sharp cracks giving way to heavier, wetter sounds. The collapse of a human head beaten against the frozen forest floor.

Chapter 36

Dr. Hill:

How have the mornings been?

Mara:

Not great. Twice this week I didn't make it to class. Barely slept but woke up late somehow. I sat on the bed with my shoes on, ready to go anyway, and just... didn't. I emailed in sick. It was the easiest lie. Said I had a migraine.

Dr. Hill:

Classic. What actually stopped you?

Mara:

The thought of walking in late.
Everyone staring. My chest felt
tight before I even left. My legs
were jittery, like they wanted
to run.

Dr. Hill:

Run from what?

Mara:

Nothing. Embarrassment? That's
the stupid part. There was no
danger. Just people in chairs.

Dr. Hill:

Yet your body acted like
there was.

Mara:

It's pathetic.

Dr. Hill:

It's ancient. May I share a
perspective?

Mara:

Sure.

Dr. Hill:

The second your brain catches a
flicker of threat, it fires an alarm.
You don't get to vote on it. That
alarm tells your body, "Get ready
right now."

Mara:

My heart was going crazy.

Dr. Hill:

Your heart speeds up to pump
blood into your biggest muscles.
Your breathing gets sharp so
more oxygen floods in. Blood
drains from your skin and
stomach to fuel your arms and
legs.

Mara:

Which is why I feel sick
sometimes.

Dr. Hill:

Right. Digestion shuts down.
Even your immune system dials
down for a moment. Your body's
pulling every bit of energy into
survival systems.

Mara:

All so I can... run away from
class?

Dr. Hill:

So you can run from anything.
Thousands of years ago, it might
have been a predator. Today, it
might be embarrassment. Social
exclusion. Your body doesn't sort
the difference well. It sees "threat"
and flips the switch.

Mara:

It feels like it makes me stupid.

Dr. Hill:

Higher thinking—planning,
reasoning—takes more time. And
time can be lethal if the danger is
real. Your body shuts that part
down for the first instant so
instinct can act fast.

Mara:

Survival of the fastest.

Dr. Hill:

Exactly. Later, when the danger
passes, thinking comes back
online. That's when you make
sense of it. But those first
seconds belong to reflex.

Mara:

And when I freeze?

Dr. Hill:

Freeze is part of the same
system. Your body slams on the
brakes, locks your muscles.
Stillness can be safer than
motion.

Mara:

It feels humiliating.

Dr. Hill:

Freeze isn't cowardice. It's
camouflage. Stillness can
convince a threat to pass you by.
Your body knows that, even if
your mind hates the feeling.

Mara:

…It feels like drowning.

Dr. Hill:

Survival doesn't ask how it feels.
It only asks if it works.

Mara:

So I can't stop this?

Dr. Hill:

You can't erase it. Fight, flight,
freeze—they're older than
speech, older than fire. You'll
never outgrow them. Therapy
can't erase them. Medication
won't either. But you can learn to
see them differently.

Mara:

Even when it ruins things? Like
missing class.

Dr. Hill:
The reflex sometimes overfires. It
triggers in safe places. That's
what this is for—not to delete it,
but to teach your body new
stories. To show it you can stay,
and nothing bad happens.

Mara:

Exposure.

Dr. Hill:
Right. Each time you stay—
without escaping—you prove to
your nervous system that fear
isn't prophecy. That staying
doesn't equal dying.

Mara:

It's hard to remember that when
my head just empties out.

Dr. Hill:
Of course. Thinking isn't gone—
it's just waiting. And every time
you ride the wave, even a little,
you teach your body a bit more
on how to handle it better.

Mara:

…Fight-or-flight is not weakness.

Dr. Hill:
Not weakness. Reflex. Design.

Mara:

I don't like it.

Dr. Hill:
You don't have to. Just know
what it is. Your body's trying to
help.

Chapter 37

Mara ran—though *ran* wasn't the right word for what her body was doing.

Snowdrifts swallowed her steps the way surf swallows a swimmer. Each stride broke against her thighs, resistance seeming to drag her backward even as she tried to push forward.

The trail itself was cruel. Twenty yards might be bare, scoured clean so her boots scraped fast across frozen dirt—and then the next stretch rose into drifts near waist-high, forcing her to almost crawl. She lurched from sprint to slog, her body never allowed one rhythm long enough to adjust. Her head always felt one second ahead of her feet, about to pitch into white.

Pain flashed through her knee. She never ran unless she was being chased. Dr. Hill had teased that out of her once. Now she felt it in her bones: She was being chased.

The storm had ended, but its ruins remained. Branches lay snapped at odd angles. Snow crusted and fissured under her step. Even the silence felt wrong— emptied, like the blizzard had stolen the forest's breath and left nothing to replace it.

Her pace dwindled to a stagger. Her pulse hammered her throat, her vision narrowing at the edges.

Stopping meant collapse.

Collapse meant death.

She forced herself on, one boot after the other.

A sign rose from the whiteness. Tilted, rimmed in frost: CLOSED. She recognized it. Willy had mentioned this spur—a shortcut back to camp, shorter by miles, but unused. Temptation flared sharp. Back to walls, to heat, to maybe some salvation.

But beside the warning, faint beneath frost, was a cave icon. Arrow pointing down the trail she was already on.

Her breath caught.

The closed path or cave ahead.

Path meant a slow, exposed route—a breadcrumb trail of footprints for Brenna to follow.

Forward meant stone, dark, the unknown.

She slowed, trembling.

The decision knotted in her chest.

She missed them. God, she missed them. Even Carl and Carly, even with their cruelty out in the open. Brenna too—quiet at the fire, leaning close, helping gather wood. Even if it had all been lies, even if the warmth had been an act, Mara longed for someone's arm across her at night. Someone to stoke the fire when her body failed.

Someone to close her eyes if she died.

Alone, she felt half erased.

She thought of Gwen—alive maybe, but not beside her. That absence carved deeper than cold. Groups decided together. A jury of survival. Now she had only herself, and she felt the danger of that: A lone vote was no vote at all.

Alone, she would perish.

Still, her legs carried her forward toward the cave arrow. Backward was death. Forward was at least hers to choose.

She hated the cleverness of it—the way the predator drove the prey. Brenna had been pushing for this trail since the crash. Always gently urging them this way, down this line of snow, toward traps they hadn't understood.

The realization burned: Brenna had been hunting them all along.

Her mind leapt further.

The snowmobiler face-down in the creek.

The dirtbiker decapitated by a cable.

Had Brenna caused those too? Was she already here, weaving the snares? The thought skittered too far—Mara pushed it away.

Trails veered faintly off left and right, spiderwebbing like dead-end options. Her focus narrowed to the air around her—the strange weight of nearness.

Then she felt it: the cave.

Not seen yet, but sensed. The trees thinned. The air changed—damp, mineral, faintly metallic. The scent of stone. The ground sloped, funneling her. She felt as though the earth itself was opening a mouth.

She was close.

A snap cracked through the trees. Sharp. Dry.

She startled so hard her knees buckled, pitching her off the trail.

Mara plunged into a hollow she hadn't seen, landing hard on her hip. Snow folded over her. Ice shot down the back of her neck. She slapped blindly at it, breath already jagged. Smothered.

Another sound. Crunch. Quick, then slowing, then quick again.

She flattened herself, burrowed, chest scraping down to frozen soil under the drift. Her pulse thudded so loud inside her hood that for a moment it mimicked footsteps. Her own body betrayed her—every heartbeat echoing like a hunter's tread.

But then the real sound came: a branch popping under weight.

Close.

She tried to push deeper, pressing her face into snow until the cold burned her eyelids. The urge was ancient and unstoppable. Cover yourself. Disappear. Become nothing. The drift pressed over her like a shallow grave.

She carved a tiny pocket of air with a tilt of her head, just enough to breathe. The snow glowed faintly above, lit by the world outside. Her only lifeline.

She tried not to breathe hard, but her lungs demanded it. Each exhale sent a cloud of warm vapor into the pocket, fogging it before thinning. She prayed it didn't seep upward. A rising wisp could betray her—all it would take was one thread of steam curling through the snow for her to be found.

Inside the drift, sound became monstrous. The scrape of fabric, the hiss of air through her teeth, even the twitch of her jaw echoed like metal. Her pulse hammered so loud she wanted to scream just to drown it out.

Now she understood. Fight-or-flight wasn't metaphor. It was this—this frantic impossibility of stillness when everything inside her screamed to move.

Outside, another snap. Closer.

Not her heart.

Not her hood.

Powder dumped over her face and sealed her mouth.

She froze, but her muscles quivered. A single tear squeezed free, freezing on her lashes.

The silence stretched wide.

Then: *crunch.*

Snow shifting above her again. Slow. Deliberate.

Steps.

Circling.

Hunting.

If she moved, the drift would collapse. If she breathed too loudly, vapor would rise or she'd be seen. Even the frantic beat of her heart felt like confession.

Another crack overhead.

Right above her.

So close, she thought. To the cave. To being found.

The glow above her flickered. A shadow passing—or just her breath clouding the air pocket. She couldn't tell. Couldn't separate hunter from heartbeat.

Either way, discovery was seconds away.

Chapter 38

She stayed buried in the snow until her lungs felt scalded from holding still. When she finally let the breath go, it hissed between her teeth—too loud, she thought, loud enough to end her—

And yet nothing happened.

No shadow passed over the snow. No hand tore her up from the drift.

Footsteps moved on.

Fading.

Warped by cold into something stretched and unreal. Then silence dropped hard, thick enough she wondered if she'd gone deaf.

Minutes passed—long enough for her cheek to go numb. Time lost meaning when you were hunted.

The cut on her lip pulsed where she'd bitten it. At

last she dared to lift her face. The world above her was empty. Pale light, no shape.

Fresh air. She breathed.

Her chest trembled. She thought of winter animals—mice tunneling under drifts, deer crouching in hollows, wolves lying still until storms passed. Maybe hiding wasn't weakness. Maybe stillness was a survival as old as anything she'd learned from people.

She dragged herself up. Snow slid down her front in wet weights, clinging like chains, and she rolled free on hands and knees, panting. Her breath rose in long clouds that felt too loud in the muteness.

The trail stretched pale and innocent in both directions. No Brenna. No Gwen.

Her heartbeat battered the quiet. It took nearly a minute before she trusted her legs to stand. When she did, the blood surged back in a rush of needles. Every joint screamed. She hugged her arms tight, scanning the woods.

Shadows looked like movement.

Branches looked like weapons.

The storm was gone, but the woods still held the posture of aftermath—stiff, stunned, waiting to see what came next.

Then she smelled it: damp, mineral, metallic.

The cave.

Between her and that smell lay a sheet of unmarked

snow. Her prints behind her were faint thanks to wind-scour and the slope where she'd slid off the trail, but if she crossed this white span, she'd leave a clean path any predator could follow.

Still, she had no choice.

She stepped forward.

The prints bloomed behind her, painfully obvious. She tried brushing them out, sweeping sideways with her boot, but each smear only made them worse. After ten yards, she stopped trying, breath shuddering.

The trail narrowed as trees bent inward. Branches arched overhead like ribs. The air grew colder—cave-cold—even before stone appeared.

She paused and closed her eyes. For a moment she heard them all again: Gwen humming, Carl muttering, Brenna's dry cough, Carly's wet moans. Their voices warped into something almost warm. She imagined them turning toward her, beckoning her back into the circle. Pretending any of them still belonged.

Her throat pinched.

She missed them.

She hated them.

Both truths lodged in her chest like ice.

The crunch of her boots was obscene in the silence. She tried the softer snow off-trail; it swallowed her thigh, twisting her knee, dragging a sob from her throat. She stumbled back onto the path.

Exposed.

A flicker of thought seized her: What if Brenna wasn't behind? What if she was ahead? Herding her. The sign, the trail, the cave—it all felt arranged.

Her stomach turned.

Mara touched the knife she had attached to her belt —Willy's knife—its leather damp but solid. Its weight steadied her hand.

Memory unspooled backward in a sudden, awful clarity: Brenna urging them forward on that trail instead of back, her silence at the wagon, her firm navigation from the fence line to the trail—not helping, but directing.

The realization stung.

Betrayal rarely announced itself. It gathered piece by piece until, suddenly, you saw the shape it had always been carving.

The cave smell thickened: earth, iron, water.

A faint drip sounded. Not wind. Water on stone.

She moved quicker, desperate to get out of the open, but each step filled with dread. Forward meant danger. Backward meant death. The sign had offered the illusion of choice, but the trail was always going to lead them here.

Still, hope clung like frost: If she kept walking, the next shape in the snow might finally be salvation.

The branches broke apart suddenly, and she stumbled into a clearing. Her breath snagged.

The cave mouth wasn't visible yet, but she felt it—pressing on her skin, cooling the air, shifting the quiet. The space felt wrong, like the woods had paused here to make room for something older.

She heard a faint groan—stone or something inside it. Not shelter. Not safety.

A mouth.

A den.

Waiting.

Her back hit a tree. She hid in its shadow, forcing herself small. Every nerve told her to rush straight in, but instinct snapped its jaws:

Predators don't always chase.

Sometimes they wait.

She crouched, smothering her breath in her sleeve.

Minutes stretched. Nothing moved.

Finally, slowly, she stepped out.

The cave was close. She could feel it—waiting, not for anyone, but for her.

Chapter 39

Paths narrowed here. What looked open from a distance folded tight in the walking.

This morning the sky was bare for the first time in days. Mara had woken to stillness, a blue so thin it looked breakable, and sunlight that touched everything without heat—like a hand pressed through glass.

She could name colors besides gray.

Mara carried that feeling with her when she'd woken —tucked it like a match in her pocket—and at first the land allowed it.

The final trail between her and the cave lay stiff and pale ahead.

The cold here was different—not wind's bite but something older, stored in rock and rationed out. It crept back across her face as the sky narrowed.

On either side, the slopes rose steep, ribbed with stone, studded with deadfall. Snow packed into shelves between trunks, hiding ledges and hollows that would collapse if she tried them.

A rabbit might scramble up.

A fox.

Not her. Not now.

The walls *led* her toward the cave. *A fatal funnel,* she thought—the term floating up from somewhere she couldn't place. Hunting. Military. Something about being trapped but not dead yet.

Yes.

That's what this was.

Somewhere behind her: Brenna's voice, far off, calling for Gwen. Mara didn't look back. The coulee wouldn't show her anything useful if she did.

Whatever followed her would arrive when it arrived. The geometry of this place made that certain.

She knew Brenna was alive. She had just heard her, and had seen her on her way to murder Carl—had felt that moment of eye contact, unmistakable. Gwen, she saw too, visible farther off, not hurrying to help. Not calling out.

Gwen had stayed distant before, when Carl had fallen. Had she stayed, maybe something would've changed.

Mara wasn't sad. Not exactly. Not angry either. She

hadn't known Carl well. A man dying was sad, of course. She still had his blood on her. What gnawed at her was the principle: A tribe could have been saved if another human had only helped. That absence counted heavier than grief.

She paused, chest heaving. Exhausted. *Scared.*

Mara could turn back now. Run into whatever was following her. Accept Brenna's arms or face what they held. Carl's head collapsing under the branch flashed through her mind, sharp as the blow itself.

A small, raw sound escaped her—half sob, half laugh at the absurdity. She pressed a pair of bare fingers to her eyes, but it didn't stop the tears.

The coulee had no mercy.

She stood one breath longer.

Then stepped forward again.

Toward Moonmilk Cavern.

The approach felt steeper than it was. Her thighs burned as if she were climbing. The shadowed mouth stayed the same size for longer than it should have, as if she walked without gaining ground.

Then the angle shifted, and the cave was there.

She looked down. The snow at the threshold in front of her bore no recent prints. No paw. No hoof. No human tread. The crust here had the preserved stillness of something waiting.

For a moment, her mind flickered back to the fire

circle—the faint warmth of the group. Now there was nothing. No group left. Just her marking the snow alone, a solitary cut in untouched white.

The one who hunted her would know she was here.

Chapter 40

The cave mouth looked less like an entrance than a warning.

A chain-link fence stretched across it, the gate thrown wide years ago, padlock corroded until rust had eaten the teeth smooth. The gate sagged from its hinges in a permanent yawn. A smaller, equally rusted chain was strung across the opening—as if an honor system had been chosen long after locks stopped mattering.

Someone had left it open on purpose, then hung a chain anyway—permission disguised as warning.

Above it, a small orange bulb burned inside a caged fixture, the kind used in mines and service tunnels. It sputtered faintly, haloed with dust and grime. The tin placard beneath had peeled almost clean, but the stenciled words still clung: EAST ENTRANCE.

Beside it hung another sign, bolted askew, patches of faded blue paint refusing to let go: Moonmilk Cavern – Authorized Access Only. The words hit her like a memory of where they'd been heading—back before the wreck, before death had begun stripping them away one by one.

The storm had passed. Outside, the air stood crisp and bare, the sky a thin blue after days of whiteout. It should have felt like relief. But as Mara scanned the clearing and tree line, she felt none.

Brenna was out there—circling, watching.

The thought knifed through her. Her chest tightened. Standing exposed was foolish. The clear light painted her like a target.

She ducked beneath the chain.

The air changed at once. Damp, mineral-heavy, with a faint sweetness like wet iron. Cave air—stone breathing around her, thick enough to swallow.

It was warmer too.

Inside was dark—dark, but not absolute. A path of bulbs stretched ahead, strung twenty feet apart along one wall, the weak glow from each only proving how vast the shadows were between. Each cage hummed faintly, lighting a small patch of slick limestone before surrendering again to black.

She moved forward, boots scuffing carefully, one hand trailing the wall. Leaving each pool of light felt like stepping off a ledge; the dark folded around her like a body pressing down. The next bulb always blasted her eyes as if she'd stepped into a spotlight—then vanished again.

Dark to dim, dim to dark—each transition painted strange colors across her vision. Pale greens, violet flares, halos pulsing like eyes opening and closing. At times it looked like smoke drifted through her sight, though she knew it was just her retinas clawing. Still, it unnerved her.

Willy's face flickered once.

Her mother—red, drunk.

Phantoms rising, then gone.

Her hand lifted without thinking to the back of her skull. Fingers pressed the matted hair where she'd bled. A bolt of pain shot through her vision, tilting the whole cave as if the darkness itself had shifted. She jerked her hand away, heart pounding. No blood on her fingers. No fresh wound. Not yet.

She thought of the others—Carly's ruined arm, Carl's stiff hand, Brenna's smashed ear—and how all of them had dragged broken bodies forward only to be swallowed anyway. Carly. Carl. Willy. Three dead. Murdered. For what? Futility etched into each body.

Her jaw locked. She would not be next. Not here.

Dr. Hill's voice whispered from her memory: *What is it about the dark that troubles you, Mara?* She had told him it wasn't not seeing that scared her—it was not being seen. That the dark erased her, swallowed her whole, left no witness she had ever been.

But now, crossing from glow to glow, she felt another truth. The dark didn't just erase her. It hid whatever else waited. Not seeing, not being seen. Erased or exposed. Either way, she lost.

At first the cave seemed silent. After two days of blizzard—the banshee wind, the hiss of snow, branches groaning overhead—the absence was shocking. Her ears rang with phantom storm noise so loud she kept expecting it to break through the rock. But the cave held only her breath: ragged, scraping, embarrassingly loud. Silence pressed tighter than the wind ever had, making her pulse feel indecent.

Then came the hidden sounds—drips landing in unseen pools, a groan deep below where stone shifted on stone. Each amplified until it felt like something exhaling beside her ear.

Not bludgeoning like the storm—intimate.

The blizzard had made her feel small; the cave made her feel seen through. Exposed inside something alive.

She reached a junction box bolted to the wall, a laminated map screwed above it. Her finger traced crude lines: a half-doughnut loop, two entrances close to the surface linked by a single curved tunnel. Narrow veins branched off—service spurs, research shafts, unlit tours long since abandoned. Faded warnings marked them: Restricted. Unlit. Science Use Only.

She saw the cave as a body. The loop a stomach. The spurs—intestines. She was inside something that could digest her.

The light here buzzed faint and orange. She lingered too long. Moving forward meant another plunge into black. She drew a breath and stepped away.

Her eyes betrayed her again—smoke, faces, colors. The dark wasn't blank. It was crowded.

And then the irony struck. Her whole life she'd feared the dark because it erased her. But here, the dark could erase her from others. Light framed her like prey on a stage. The shadows swallowed everything else.

The dark might consume her—but it could also hide her.

That thought gnawed at her as she slipped from glow to glow, no longer drawn to light but measuring distance by it. Her boots slid on wet limestone. Steps carved shallow and slick. She tested each with her good leg. Her bad one trembled.

Halfway down the second set, it failed.

Her boot skidded on the wet lip. Her knee twisted. Pain seared so hot she screamed.

The sound cracked the cave open, ricocheting in a dozen ghostly versions of itself. Echoes layered and warped until it wasn't hers anymore—prey sound, carrying.

Brenna will hear that, she thought. *Anyone will.*

Then silence clamped down—sharp, listening.

She froze, clutching the iron rail, cheek smacking wet stone. The cave smelled of rust and mineral.

Her blood hammered in her ears.

Pain swelled until thought shredded. Her vision sparked. Lips tingled. Limbs went slack. She slid sideways into the wall, body slumping into shadow.

She used to wonder how people could pass out from physical pain. Now she understood.

Black pressed close. Dimly, she realized: She had fallen into dark shadows. Cover. If someone followed, they might pass without seeing her.

Good, she thought. The dark she'd feared—it could erase her, yes, but it might also save her. Prey survived when predators believed them gone.

Prey.

Was she prey?

Her last breath slipped out shallow and weak.

The cave tilted. Sound faded, as though she were sinking underwater—breath, pulse, thought—dissolving into black.

And then there was nothing.

Chapter 41

Dr. Hill:
You look shaken. The dream again?

Mara:
Yeah. Same one. Back where I grew up. Rural road, woods cleared for new houses. They're digging foundations. And I panic because I'm certain I buried someone there—no name, no time, just the conviction of it. The dream doesn't explain. I just know I helped hide it. And if they keep building, they'll find it.

Dr. Hill:
And you wake half convinced it's real.

Mara:

More than half. I lie there making
lists of who it could be. Which is
insane, because I've never killed
anyone.

Dr. Hill:

The dream isn't about fact. It's
about fear.

Mara:

Fear of going crazy. Fear of losing
control so badly I do something
out of character, unforgivable.

Dr. Hill:

That fear is common. More
common than most people admit.
People fear they'll stab someone
just because a knife is in reach.
Or drive into oncoming traffic. Or
throw a baby off a balcony.
Almost always, those thoughts
don't mean danger. They mean
the opposite.

Mara:

That I care.

Dr. Hill:

That you care. Worry is proof of
value. You panic about hurting
because you don't want to hurt.
The mind's cruel trick is to show
you the worst picture of what you
won't allow, to remind you how
much it matters.

Mara:

Then why does it feel so
convincing? If I can imagine it,
doesn't that mean it's inside me?

Dr. Hill:

It means you're imaginative. That
your brain rehearses catastrophe
to keep you alert. It's a fire drill
that keeps sounding even after
the building's been checked.

Mara:

But I see it. I feel it. The dirt under
my nails, the weight of it in the
ground.

Dr. Hill:

Because your brain doesn't
separate image from act as
cleanly as you think. Dreams can
feel real enough to brand memory.
But recall: No body has been
buried. Only fear. That's what lies
underground.

Mara:

Still feels sick.

Dr. Hill:

It's human. Panic is the body's
alarm system running too hot. A
person with panic and a knife in
their hand isn't the threat. They're
the one suffering. The threat is the
person who holds the knife with
no panic, no second thought.
Choice. Violence is almost always
chosen, Mara. Not slipped into by
accident.

Mara:

But people do snap. They
go mad.

Dr. Hill:

Rarely. We claim killers "snap"
because it comforts us more than
the truth. It implies they weren't in
control. But most were.
Deliberate, aware, eyes open.
Ever possible? Yes. Probable?
No. Panic doesn't create violence.
Choice does.

Mara:

I'm fighting shadows.

Dr. Hill:

Good way to put it. Panic is a
shadow—convincing, shaped like
danger, but nothing behind it.
That's what panic is: an echo in
the dark, as convincing as breath
at your ear.

> **Mara:**
>
> I wish someone had handed me a
> knife sooner.

Dr. Hill:

Why?

> **Mara:**
>
> Because then I'd have known. I
> would've been flooded with the
> truth that I wasn't going to stab
> Sophie. Or anyone. All that
> wasted panic, all those nights... I
> would've seen it: that my fear
> meant control. That I was safe
> from myself.

Dr. Hill:

Sometimes it takes proximity to
prove distance.

> **Mara:**
>
> But isn't it also true? Under the
> right circumstances... anyone
> could kill.

Dr. Hill:

Of course. Could you stab someone, Mara? Or help bury a body? Absolutely. You and every other human on earth. Strip away enough safety, add enough pressure, enough survival logic— yes. We're built for it. That's not panic, though. That's choice.

Mara:
Choice.

Dr. Hill:

Humans can do things they never thought possible—but almost always because they decided to. Maybe grimly, maybe reluctantly, maybe with rationalizations stacked to the ceiling, but still: decided. You're confusing that with your panic disorder, which is a completely different animal. Panic is a false fire alarm. It blares when nothing is burning. Murder is not a false alarm.

Mara:
So I'm not secretly dangerous.

Dr. Hill:

No. You're not a murderer, and you're not going to spontaneously become one. You've been living with panic disorder, Mara—and you've fought it hard. What you're afraid of is a phantom: the idea that terror itself could make you violent. That isn't how it works. Fight-or-flight—sometimes freeze —those are the reflexes panic summons. An urge to flee because you fear you might harm someone isn't proof of danger. It's the opposite. It's proof of conscience.

Mara:

But it feels so twisted. Like I'm afraid of me.

Dr. Hill:

It is paradoxical, and it's awful. Panic convinces you the threat is in your own hands, your own mind. So you try to flee yourself— and of course you can't. That's what makes it so cruel. Panic isn't pointing at knives or cliffs. It's pointing at you. But again: That's not compulsion. It's the body misfiring its alarm.

Mara:

So even with a knife in my hand,
panic doesn't make me
dangerous.

Dr. Hill:

No. If anything, panic makes you
safer than most. You'll shake,
sweat, maybe even drop the
knife. You won't choose violence
because of it. Panic incapacitates
or drives escape. Violence comes
from choice.

Mara:

Choice…

"Suffering is not the enemy; it is the gate."
Dōgen

Chapter 42

Mara woke to her own groan, cheek still pressed against wet stone. For a long moment, she couldn't tell if she was lying flat or falling—the dizziness was so thick it blurred her sense of up from down.

Pain pulsed from her skull in waves, sharp enough to wash her vision gray. Her knee flared hot as fire beneath her, every twitch sending barbed jolts up into her hip.

She rolled halfway onto her side, breath whistling through clenched teeth. One palm slid along the cave wall until she found its roughness anchoring her— steady, cold, real. She stayed there, spine pressed to stone, waiting as her head throbbed.

The cave hummed around her: the faint buzz of a junction box somewhere nearby, a slow drip of water striking rock in patient rhythm. She let those sounds tether her until the nausea ebbed.

When she finally reached for the railing she remembered crossing, her hand found it slick. She gripped hard and dragged herself upright, swaying, eyes shut. A full minute passed before her legs felt anything like trustworthy.

She had no idea how long she'd been down. Minutes, hours—her skull held nothing but pain. She fumbled for Willy's knife, tugging it free as if the blade might carry some measure of time. Its surface showed only her own pale face, warped in steel. No clock. No clue. She let her gaze rake the walls, the junction box, the faint bulbs overhead, as if any of them might tell her what she'd lost. Ridiculous. Hopeless.

The cave kept its secrets.

Her knee burned—a furnace in miniature. Her head felt split, her skull stuffed with light. But it was her thirst that tore at her most. Dryness coated her tongue, her throat tight as sand. She thought of a half-empty canteen, melted snow shared among too many hands. Of the few powdery mouthfuls she'd eaten along the trail— cold that stabbed her teeth. Not enough. Not even close.

She staggered forward.

That was when she saw it.

The walls gleamed. Rippling bands of pale mineral,

whipped and crusted as if sugar had been dragged in sweeping strokes across black stone.

Moonmilk.

She'd heard Willy name it once, in passing, but she had never seen it. Now it glowed faintly in the weak spill of the bulbs, as though the rock had frozen starlight into its skin.

"...Oh wow," she whispered—her voice small, humbled.

For a breath, she forgot the ache in her knee. The bulbs caught in the white crust and scattered light in soft halos. It was fragile, otherworldly—like walking inside the ribcage of a sleeping star.

And in that glow, something stirred inside her she hadn't expected: awe. Even here, hunted and broken, she could still stop for beauty. Humans always had— scraping art onto cave walls, telling stories beside fire-light, clinging to meaning even as the world closed in. Maybe survival wasn't just food or warmth, but the will to notice beauty and let it move you, if only for a moment.

Something else shimmered—a faint, shifting reflection. She turned, squinting. Not light. Water.

A small pool had gathered at the cave's base, still enough to shine back the bulb's glow.

She scrambled toward it, dropping to her knees despite the fire that flared in her leg. She plunged her hands into the pool and brought water to her lips—cold enough to bite. It was the most delicious thing she had ever tasted. She drank until her belly swelled, and when she finally pulled back, she pressed both hands to the stone, fighting nausea.

A flicker of fear crossed her mind—what if it wasn't clean, what if it poisoned instead of saved?—but desperation overruled.

It might poison her.

She drank more anyway.

She thought fleetingly that Brenna would drink from the same pool if she found it. Gwen too. The thought unsettled her. They could hate, betray, even kill—but all of them still bent to the same thirst. Survival bound them, no matter how splintered they were.

When the cramps came, she closed her eyes and breathed through them, waiting for the sickness to settle.

Minutes passed before she could stand.

When she moved on, she found a rhythm. A limp, angled carefully so her weight landed more on her good leg, sparing the worst of her ruined knee. Not graceful—but it worked. Step, drag, brace. Step, drag, brace. Enough to keep going.

She passed a spur marked with a battered sign, arrow pointing downward. For an instant, she imagined following it—descending deeper into the earth, curling into a warm pocket where no storm or hunter could reach. A burrow. A refuge. But she had no light of her own. And if she'd blacked out here where she had light, she would not survive the unlit shafts below.

So she stayed with the loop.

The rhythm carried her until sound broke it.

She froze.

At first she thought it was an echo—the slap of her own boot, delayed. But that wasn't right. Echoes returned instantly, stretched thin by space. This was slower. A beat behind. Her steps, answered by something else.

She stood still, heart hammering. The cave answered her stillness with its own.

She forced herself forward again, testing. Step, drag, brace.

And there it was. Another step. Not hers. Not timed to her limp—but following it.

Her mind flickered—head injury, hallucination, nerves jangling after days of storm and blood. She almost convinced herself.

Almost.

Then she saw it.

Ahead, where one bulb hummed against stone, a figure darted across the spill of light. Quick. Careful. There and gone. Too tall to be Carly. Too lean to be Carl. Not Gwen. The shoulders were wrong, the gait too sharp.

Brenna? It had to be.

Mara melted into darkness.

She crouched low, spine curved forward, limbs tucked, every nerve alive with the old, ancestral knowledge Dr. Hill had once spoken of. The dark terrified her —erasure, annihilation, the place where she ceased to exist. But it was also cover. Cloak. Both truths pressed into her, twin poisons in her chest.

She hated it—and she needed it.

Mara slowed her breath, spread it thin, let her chest move less than a whisper. Her body trembled from the effort but she held still, almost animal.

The light ahead buzzed—faint, orange—and through it the figure moved again. Closer now. Close enough she could see the tilt of a head, the deliberate pause of someone listening.

Mara did not breathe.

And in the dark, she waited.

Chapter 43

The figure drew nearer, stumbling in and out of the weak glow of the bulbs.

At first Mara had thought it was Brenna—lithe, a shadow too steady to be harmless. Her chest tightened, heart hammering.

But then the figure lurched sideways, catching herself against the wall. Thin. Uneven. Streaks of blood down one cheek.

Gwen.

The storm had ended hours ago, but the new silence clung to everything. The sky above the world was clear now, the blizzard gone. Here underground, the real weather was people.

Mara broke from the dark. She rushed forward, boots scraping stone, colliding with Gwen before she could think. The impact slammed them both into the damp wall. Gwen clutched her with desperate, shaking hands, sobs tearing loose from her chest.

"Mara—" Her voice cracked, rasped, splintered. "Oh God. I thought I was finished. I thought—" She buried her face against Mara's shoulder, breath hot and ragged.

"She saw me come in. Brenna did. I know she saw me."

The words spilled, frantic and disordered. Then Gwen lifted her face, eyes red and wet, searching Mara's with something naked and childlike.

"We're together," she whispered. "Finally. I'm not alone."

Mara's throat tightened. Her own voice came out small, almost tender. "No. You're not alone."

Yet even as she spoke, Mara felt the imbalance—the way Gwen had walked away when others stayed, had chosen herself while the group broke apart around them. She thought of Carl bleeding in the pit, Carly screaming through her ruined arm, Willy cut open. All of them had carried each other until they couldn't anymore.

Gwen had left.

And now she returned, clutching at Mara like a drowning swimmer.

Mara's hand moved—stroking Gwen's shoulder, her hair—and then lower. Gwen had left the circle. And circles don't survive betrayal.

Her fingers closed around the knife's handle.

Cool. Certain.

And then Mara stabbed her.

A single thrust. Swift. Upward. Inevitable.

The blade slid beneath Gwen's jaw, parting soft flesh before punching through the base of her tongue. Her mouth dropped open, steel jutting grotesquely upward, pressing against the hard palate.

For a heartbeat, it seemed to lodge there—straining—before Mara drove it higher.

A muffled pop echoed in Gwen's skull as the point broke through. Her lips quivered around the intrusion—then her jaw snapped shut.

Her eyes froze wide.

Her body jolted.

Once. Twice.

Mara yanked the knife free in a single downward pull. Gwen collapsed instantly, sliding down Mara's arms until she sprawled on the cold stone.

Blood spread fast, warm, pooling across the floor until it touched the pale ridges of moonmilk. The white mineral seemed to drink it, edges glowing deep red. Light refracted, painting the cavern walls in fractured panes of white and crimson—

A cathedral of bleeding stone.

Mara knelt there, steady. Her chest shook, but her hands did not.

This was no accident. No frenzy. She had meant it. Intended it. Chose it.

Gwen's return had carried its own indictment—abandoning when others fought to hold together, then clutching at Mara as if that break hadn't mattered.

The knife wasn't punishment or cruelty.

It was principle. Values carried out in steel.

Dr. Hill had once said survival required compromise, that you couldn't always live by principle. But she hadn't believed him.

Not then.

Not now.

Mara breathed once—deep, slow, steady.

This was her. Choosing. Acting. In control of every motion. Beauty and ruin in the same stroke.

She was doing so well.

Chapter 44

Mara set the knife gently beside Gwen's body and reached for a rock the size of a softball. Smooth.

Heavy.

Honest.

It fit her palm with the primitive certainty of something older than tools, older than language. A rock was what humans used before they had names for their weapons. Before knives. Before fire.

Gwen's death, she reminded herself, wasn't only principle. It was practical. There were only a few paths out of this alive, and Gwen—cling-on, inconsistent, reflexively loyal to whoever held her up—would have exposed her sooner or later. Survival wasn't always the strongest enduring. Sometimes it was removing the ones who would drag the rest down.

Mara reclaimed her cheap mittens.

Pulled them from Gwen's dead hands.

She moved toward the exit Gwen had come through, careful on the damp stone. The dark pressed close. Humans weren't built for this: not for blind movement.

We break ourselves so easily in the dark.

She had never met Gwen properly before all this, nor any of them, but she'd heard enough: fragments when Dr. Hill ran late, whispers among staff about "poor Gwen," about the chaos of Carl and Carly. Gwen had always been someone attached to someone else, never standing alone. And when Mara got into her therapy notes—it had all made sense.

Brenna wasn't going to kill Gwen, who was the spitting image of pathology to Brenna's dead sister. Brenna would happily slaughter anyone, it would seem. But not Gwen.

Mara knew this. Knew there was no way that Mara *and* Gwen both walked out of this alive. Maybe if Gwen hadn't broken the circle or had helped her get Carl out of the pit. But she hadn't. She'd left.

At the mouth of the cave, Mara braced herself, rock tucked behind her back with both hands. She expected a rush from the trees—Brenna charging like some furious animal, branch club raised for a bludgeoning.

Nothing came. At first.

Minutes passed. The clearing held its breath.

For a fleeting moment, Mara wondered if Brenna had stumbled into one of her own snares. The thought warmed her with a strange, buoyant relief.

Then she saw the eyes.

Straight ahead. Wide. Luminous. Catching what little light the winter day allowed.

Beautiful. Hypnotic. The same eyes that had burned into hers by the fire—gold and blue in shadow, startling in their focus.

She hated that her body couldn't tell terror from desire. Both surged from the same place. Both left her trembling. Brenna's eyes made her feel hunted—and some part of her wanted to be.

Brenna stepped forward, her shape forming out of the trees. She had dropped the branch. Apparently. A knife hung from her hand instead.

Unexpected.

Mara had brought a rock to a knife fight. The absurdity nearly amused her—primitive versus refined, beginning versus end. She smiled at Brenna, feeling the pull of the moment.

There was a fresh cut along Brenna's face, just under the eye—small, imperfect, the kind of wound made by someone desperate and outmatched. Carl, she realized. He didn't see the truth beneath the size, behind the softness of Brenna. Not until it was too late.

When Brenna was only a few feet away, quickening, Mara spoke. Calm. Clear.

"Michelle."

The name struck like a thrown stone. Brenna faltered—softened—confusion and recognition blooming where murderous focus had lived.

Names had weight. They reminded. They accused. They dragged people back into selves they thought they'd shed.

The knife dipped a fraction.

That was all Mara needed.

Mara's arm swung. The rock smashed into Brenna's face with a wet crack, jerking her sideways. She collapsed in the snow, knife still clutched.

No frenzy. No wasted motion.

Mara knelt, raised the rock with both hands, and brought it down twice. The first blow flattened Brenna's cheek. The second caved in the orbit of her eye, bone folding inward into brain with a faint squishy pop.

Enough.

She stood, wiped the mess from her sleeve, and looked down at what had been *Michelle*.

Relief didn't come.

Something colder did.

This wasn't prey defending itself.

This was choice—deliberate, curated death.

Survival shaped by Mara's own hand.

From the body, she took the coat and the phone. Adjusted the hood. Pulled her repatriated mittens tight. She turned toward the shorter trail. Five miles, she estimated, maybe less.

Haunted or not.

She started walking.

Chapter 45

The land widened again, undoing what it had done on her way in. No longer a throat, no longer ribs narrowing around her—just open slopes and a thin wash of milk-blue sky.

Her boots scuffed over snow. She slowed.

Running parallel to her own tracks was a second line —smaller, lighter. Michelle had followed her prints to the cave. Petite feet ghosting beside hers, almost step for step.

Seeing them now, after everything, chilled her.

She had never been alone. Not really.

As she stepped onto the shorter forbidden trail— Willy's trail, the one he'd warned them from—she felt a thin ache for him.

Mara was a killer now.

She hadn't been when she met Willy.

Mara had seen him from the trees where she'd squatted to piss their first night outside, while she was crying like an embarrassed hiker out of her depth.

She saw Willy, striding off alone to find the road, to call for help. Then she had seen Michelle (Brenna) following him.

Mara shadowed her, curious whether the thing she feared most was about to happen. And in some awful private place, it was the thing she'd hoped might happen.

Michelle paused once to listen, then kept walking, following Willy's footprints.

Mara stayed where she was—absolutely still, barely breathing—letting the woods close around her. If she moved too soon, she might change the shape of whatever was coming.

So she waited.

Cold, hidden, complicit by stillness.

Then it happened.

Willy heard Michelle approaching but wasn't ready. From a distance, Mara watched her swing—a sharp blow to the side of his head—then another as he fell.

Two more strikes. One to the skull, and one after she rolled him over, collapsing his throat with the branch she'd carried like a pilgrim's staff.

It was over in moments.

And Brenna the Bludgeoner—*Michelle*—slipped silently back toward camp.

Only then did Mara step forward.

Willy was too heavy to hoist the way she'd imagined. But she managed what she could.

Mara took his knife.

The work was messy at first—strings of sinew resisting parting—but by the end it became almost clean.

Like working on a doll: awkward, clumsy, frightening only until repetition dulled it. Then, oddly satisfying.

She wiped Willy's blade clean and put it back in his satchel where she'd found it.

The next day—the look on Michelle's face when they found the man she had murdered, mutilated and displayed by someone else—

Was exquisite.

The trail forked. The shorter spur dipped steeply, her knee answering with a jolt like a hammer to the joint. Willy's warning surfaced—*We don't take that route.* Then he'd died anyway, skull split under Michelle's branch, throat sealed shut.

His warnings hadn't saved him.

She eyed the spur. Cursed or not, she was taking it.

"Watch your step," she muttered. "Michelle went a little wild on the *Home Alone* routine."

The snow turned treacherous. Wind had carved

bowls into the path, then half refilled them with porcelain crust. Every few steps, the surface broke and pitched her forward; every few it held, forcing her body to guess. Her knee hated guessing. It wanted the predictable ground of a life she no longer had.

Her breath rose like stage smoke. The storm had fully withdrawn, leaving only a thin wind combing the trees and the bronze rattle of oak leaves clinging through the last of winter.

When the group had been alive, that sound had passed for conversation. Now it echoed like an empty house.

Michelle. The name tasted like aspirin. Brenna had never been Brenna at all. Mara remembered first seeing the birth name Michelle in Dr. Hill's paperwork—tucked between intake notes and treatment goals. *Michelle*, clinical and unadorned. She had traced her in threads online later, each confirming the file's whisper.

The details were grotesque. Parents so cruel it read like fiction. A sister caged for much of her childhood. Michelle beaten when she tried to help. Dr. Hill had once called it "flexibility"—the ability to bend without breaking. That same flexibility had carried Michelle through the Driftless, where kindness became camouflage and branches became weapons.

Mara's breath hitched, almost a laugh.

Again the thought: Could the dirtbiker Willy

described—the one decapitated by a cable stretched across the trail—have been Michelle's handiwork? An early Driftless exposure exercise? The idea thrilled her with its terrible symmetry. The kind of symmetry no one could prove now that Michelle lay ruined in the snow.

Her knee flared as the spur steepened. She palmed a trunk for balance, listened to the bare branches clatter their muted applause. Gwen's face flashed in memory— raw, desperate, hands clutching too tight. The circle broken. The tribe shattered.

Practicality had demanded Gwen's removal just as it had required Michelle's. Mara had known since Willy that the only one safe from the killer stalking them in the woods was Gwen.

Mara tugged her hood low and pressed on. The trail bent again, sloping her toward the open. Each step felt less like escape and more like continuation—forward into the outcome she'd already chosen.

At the top of the nature trail, the black cube of a cabin emerged through the thinning trees.

She stopped.

When she'd taken this path down, there had been six of them—laughter, muttering, breath rising in one shared cloud.

Now there was only her.

She looked back, because humans always looked back at the places that had changed them.

The coulees lay quiet, steep and white, the Driftless holding everything that had happened and refusing to give any of it back.

No fire. No tribe.

No circle.

Just her, moving on.

Chapter 46

By the time she reached her car and turned the ignition, the dash clock read just shy of 4:00 p.m. Early, all things considered. She let the engine run, then opened Sophie's lockbox and collected her bag and phone.

The cabin was hers for another night, but she wouldn't need it.

And lingering wasn't wise.

Outside, the storm was still gone; the cold had cracked open. Air pressed heavy and damp, thick with scent: thawing soil, pine warming to pitch, the faint iron tang of old blood leaching into slush. Water rattled from branches, ran in sudden seams across the road. The snow that had sealed them in sagged and sloughed, collapsing under its own melt.

The whole world seemed to be undoing itself—edges softening, lines running.

She decided to drive without GPS.

No signal anyway. She thought she remembered the turns back to the highway.

She'd manage.

On the road, Mara reflected on the chalk lines of her experiment. Dr. Hill liked to send patients here alone— for exposure, for reflection. Never overlapping. Privacy mattered to him.

But Mara had always been a snoop.

A curator of people's stories and how to use them.

Michelle's trauma lay plain in the therapy transcripts: a sister caged and humiliated by their parents. Pair that with Gwen's therapy story—gossip Mara had first overheard at reception—and the fit was seamless.

The bait irresistible.

Mara had known Michelle had a taste for bludgeoning, that she'd killed before in ways highly brutal. Her age and circumstances had been the only reason she wasn't in prison. What Mara hadn't known—what no file or online grooming could prepare her for—was how far Michelle would go once given the stage.

Grooming, Mara thought—despite the sourness of the word—had never been mystical. It only sounded that way because people preferred myths to mechanics, and because the people most often caught doing it were men with the luxury of cover.

It wasn't charm. It wasn't seduction.

It was information and time. Listening long enough to learn what someone feared, then offering relief shaped exactly to fit.

There was no master plan beyond getting Michelle primed and present here with them.

That was the funny part.

Mara had lingered too long in her therapist's office. Read what she wasn't meant to. Then fed Michelle facts—Carl's cruelty, Carly's rot—never pushing, never insisting. Just listening. Letting anger stretch. Letting imagination do the work.

She shared where Gwen and the Fenwicks would be this weekend.

Then Mara signed up herself.

Showed up. Stayed present.

Worked on her anxiety.

Michelle overdelivered. Pitfalls. Moonmilk. A slaughterhouse dressed as wilderness.

Mara had prepared for the possibility of nothing happening. That, more than anything, had felt like the risk. She had hoped but not expected to see Michelle. Who'd gone dark online a week earlier. Mara assumed the anger had burned out—or found another target.

It hadn't.

Mara smiled, imagining Michelle scavenging the countryside in a borrowed backhoe with stolen materials —coils of wire lifted without permission from neighboring farms.

Quiet trespasses.

The kind of preparation that felt intimate.

Clever, impressive woman, Mara thought.

The melt blurred into pale streaks along the road. Her knee burned, of course it did. Swollen stiff, refusing to bend. Each time she shifted on the pedal, her whole leg screamed, hot and sharp.

It frightened her in a way the traps, the knives, the storm hadn't—not panic but permanence.

The certainty that her knee would never be the same.

That *she* would never be the same.

And yet somehow, that thought also steadied her.

The walk back to camp had been long, slow. She'd staggered more than once, her body wrecked in ways she hadn't fully registered.

Peg-leg Mara, she thought.

Thrown from a tractor, bashed in the head, tripped over more stumps than she could count. Her feet raw and soggy, maybe frostbitten. Her body a ledger of bruises and blunt trauma.

She laughed out loud at the absurdity.

Mara wondered if that was what the monks carried

—the few who made it out—scars in flesh and spirit, pain fused to enlightenment. Afraid, yes. Changed, yes. But altered into something far rarer.

Strangest of all: She wasn't anxious. Not anymore. And the nights—she'd slept better these last three nights, ironically, than she had in years.

Maybe ever.

The world outside the windshield felt different. Sharper. Diesel, pine, the faint iron tang of her own blood. Or maybe someone else's. What had once overwhelmed her now came through clear.

At the first truck stop, she pulled in, numb with injury and cold. She'd never showered in a place like that before. Never would have. Now it felt simple. Pleasant. She scrubbed away days of blood and dirt, patched what cuts she could reach.

The mirror startled her—lacerations along her cheek, a head wound worse than she'd realized, hair matted thick. Bruises everywhere.

Concussion?

Hypothermia and concussion rules said naps were bad. Don't sleep. She smiled crookedly and winked at herself. *Guess I'm out of the woods on that one.*

Literally.

She bought a tuna sandwich and dill pickle chips. Ate them in the lot, salt on her fingers, not minding the cheapness.

Food tasted real again.

Exhaustion pressed heavy on her chest, but beneath it was something steadier, clearer. She had bled, vomited, run for her life. Survived pitfalls, frost, and a capable killer.

Her doing, yes.

But still—she had done well.

She gripped the wheel, her hands torn and red against it.

Mara understood now: Survival wasn't courage or triumph. It was the body staggering forward anyway after fear had stripped you raw.

Mara Keene, she thought. *You're tired, battered, damn near poisoned, and were almost murdered by your own creation.*

And you can't wait to do it again.

But first—a hot bath for her ruined knee.

And a session with Dr. Hill.

Would You Recommend Driftless Hollow?

If this story—or Mara Keene—stayed with you, I'd be grateful if you'd consider leaving a brief review. It doesn't have to be long—just a few words are enough.

Reviews help other readers decide whether to step into the hollow themselves. You can leave a review wherever you purchased this book, on Goodreads, or at **DreadfullyCurious.com**.

Thank you for reading.
—Ben Tor

Stay Up To Date

If you'd like to hear about my future books, releases, or related work, you can sign up for updates below.

I don't send frequent emails, and I don't share personal details—just occasional notes when there's something new to read.

You can sign up here:
BenTorAuthor.com

Until then.
—Ben Tor